ANY KIND OF BROKEN MAN

Roger Granelli was born and bred in Wales, and educated at the University of Warwick and Cardiff University. He is a writer, a professional musician and also a landscape photographer.

He has published a novella and ten novels in various genres and styles, including historical fiction to crime fiction. He has won three writing awards for his work, and has had many of his short stories published in literary magazines and broadcast on BBC Radio.

ANY KIND OF BROKEN MAN
COLLECTED STORIES

ROGER GRANELLI

Cockatrice Books

Y diawl a'm llaw chwith

First published in 2022 by Cockatrice Books
Editor: Rob Mimpriss
www.cockatrice-books.com
mail@cockatrice-books.com

Thanks are due to the editors in whose journals these stories first appeared: *New Welsh Review* ('Quiet Keith', 'Money Scoop', 'Off the Scrapheap', 'The Four Aces' and 'In the Wake of the Sun', first published under the title, 'Eduardo and Felipe'), *Planet* ('The Beached Whales', 'Tremlett's Time' and 'On Top of the World'), and *The Interpreter's House* ('Firebug'). 'Pushover' was first published in Cary Archard (ed.), *Mr Roopratna's Chocolate: The Winning Stories from the Rhys Davies Competition* (Bridgend: Seren, 2000). 'Losing It' was commissioned as a Quick Read by Accent Press in 2008, and 'Money Scoop', 'Tremlett's Time' and 'On Top of the World' were broadcast by BBC radio.

CONTENTS

FOREWORD

Italian? Jewish? Or just a damn fine writer from the Valleys...?

When I first started reading adult books, there wasn't much of a gap between popular and literary fiction. The big bestsellers, from Heller's *Catch 22* to the very British works of authors like John Fowles, were some of the best-written and most widely-read novels around.

But by the time I was compiling a book programme for BBC Radio Wales, the literary climate had changed, and the most successful Welsh storytellers, from Dick Francis to Ken Follett, were highly accomplished but not what you'd call 'literary.' Most literary writers no longer felt obliged to produce a readable story. It was not about what you wrote as much as how you wrote it, and a quality novel was usually a challenge to read. Any enjoyment or satisfaction often came not in reading it but in *having read it*, all the way through to what was seldom a happy or even pleasing ending.

My radio programme, however, was supposed to be about enjoyable reading, so I admit to avoiding many writers who were clearly acclaimed purely for producing elegant sentences... and being Welsh.

Granelli's novel *Status Zero* made a real impression on me

when it first came out. It didn't look at first as if it would break the new mould. It was about this nasty no-hope kid in the kind of South Wales sink estate where you learned to steal efficiently long before picking up the rudiments of reading. 'The story of an adolescent starting from a perilous position,' said the blurb, 'in a society which couldn't give a damn. Provocative, moving, it is also the story of a boy becoming a man...'

In a modern 'literary' novel, the boy would become a man just in time to realise, in a clipped paragraph of twisted irony, that it was already far too late to escape his street-level past. So, as *Status Zero* tended, instead, to fulfil our vague hopes for Mark Richards' salvation, it couldn't be 'literary', could it? It's clearly more time-consuming for a writer to construct a complex, positive conclusion than it would be to follow the story to a simple and acceptably tragic end. The longer, more sympathetic version might be more emotionally satisfying to readers but perhaps less stylish for the cooler publishers.

Status Zero was Roger Granelli's fourth full-length novel, but he'd also written a stack of short stories by then, including 'The Beached Whales,' which provided a scary coda to the Mark Richards story and served up a more 'literary' ending. Was the final appearance of Mark's small half-brother a bad dream or a worse memory?

It wasn't, however, the final appearance of Mark, who resurfaced as the central character of Granelli's later foray into genre novels. Mark was now in London, where he'd become a private investigator with a beautiful girlfriend who – always a risk for beautiful girlfriends in genre fiction – got murdered. That justified the title, *Dead Pretty,* which ended up published by mass-marketeers Headline.

This short story collection spans Granelli's whole writing career, 'Quiet Keith,' his first published story, coming out before his superb first novel, *Crystal Spirit.* Short stories gave the author room to experiment with different styles and formats, including the novella introduced by Amazon for its own publishing venture, the Kindle Single. *Pushover*, one of the first great Singles, is the story of a Holocaust survivor menaced by Cardiff street-scum and what he does about it. Like *Status Zero*, its ending satisfied readers, and it won Granelli great acclaim, one reviewer describing him as a 'promising new Jewish writer.'

Despite being born and bred in South Wales, where his Italian grandfather was in the ice-cream business, Granelli has written five convincingly-Italian Mafia novels. Set in Palermo, the series ended with *Stiletto Sisters*, all published by Amazon.

Roger Granelli has published ten novels altogether, plus 'Losing It,' his 'Quick Read,' which was translated for Norway and became a Norwegian school text for English learners. Could be time for a move into moody Scandinavian crime fiction? Coming from such a talented and versatile writer as the author of this collection, nothing need surprise us.

Phil Rickman

February 2022

LOSING IT

Other men might have lost it, lashing out against this affront to their interests and their pride, but Baldock preferred to make an impression that would last. Keep a clear head, he told himself, and soon he knew what he was going to do.

From the top window Baldock looked out over the terraces, bleak and outdated to some, but comforting to him. He liked their conformity, and the wasted remains of former glories that lay all around them. A row of abandoned factories dominated his line of vision as the sun went down on them, flashing off their rotting roofs and ruined windows. As he looked down the valley he could trace the sites of old industries, now just undulations, landscaped contours too bulbous and fresh to really blend in. A solitary pithead had been left standing, for posterity and the tourists who never came. Baldock found a kind of beauty in the scene. It was his world.

It had been a good spell. Deals had gone smoothly, all monies had been paid on time, and everyone was behaving. Apart from TJ. That boy had broken rank big time. His father's coughing brought Baldock away from the window, and out of his thoughts.

'You're like a bloody statue,' the old man said, 'standing

at the window all the time, worse than your mother ever was.'

Baldock turned to look at him, at the man enveloped in bedclothes, propped up with pillows, and looking rather shrunken in the double bed.

'You haven't eaten your food,' Baldock said.

'Don't want it. Rabbit food, that is.'

'It's what you're supposed to have.'

'What the hell does it matter what I eat now? It's as stupid as trying to get me to stop smoking.'

'Don't start that again. I'll make you a pot of tea.' Baldock took his father's tray, and rearranged the pillows. 'It's your birthday tomorrow, dad. Seventy-five.'

'And you're almost forty, and still looking out the sodding window.'

Baldock smiled. He liked the old man's temper, for it had long since lost its bite. He was a toothless old dog now.

'I'll bring the tea up in a minute. And there's boxing on the telly.'

'Boxing indeed. Not these days, it's just overweight bears dancing with each other now.'

Even so, the old man snatched up the remote and pointed it belligerently at the television, which Baldock had mounted on the wall of the bedroom for him. His father had been a decent fighter himself once.

Someone knocked the kitchen door when Baldock was making the tea. Tony, one of his runners, came in.

'You're late,' Baldock said.

'I had to wait around for the money,' the boy answered, 'you know what they're like up the site.'

'But no trouble?'

'Course not. As if.'

'What about TJ?'

'Gone to ground, since the word is out. But all the boys is looking for the git.' Baldock took the two hundred pounds from the boy, and gave him thirty back, and some more packages.

'These are for the bottom site and Friday night. Give half to Rob and tell him to get his arse over here by seven tonight.'

'Right.'

'Piss off, then.'

And the boy was gone, swiftly, gladly, which made Baldock smile for the second time that day. Power was a strange thing, a gratifying thing, and he had it in spades, its foundation laid with people's need. He rubbed the rawness of losers' lives a little redder whilst giving them a quick fix and it did not worry him at all. Suckers and even breaks never mixed, not in his world.

He took the tea up to his father before the old man had chance to knock on the floor with his stick. The television was on without the sound.

'Look at those two,' the old man muttered, 'it's like a bloody circus act. Too fat and too slow, the pair of them.'

'That's how it is now, dad. Everything is bigger in the world, including boxing.'

'Aye, I suppose it is.'

The old man's chest rippled and he went into a bout of coughing, a series of dry rapid rasps, as if his lungs were trying to tear themselves away from the dust inside them.

Baldock stood patiently with his tray, not showing undue concern. The old man did not want any; they were alike in this at least.

'Did I hear someone downstairs just then?'

'Only Tony.'

'I hope he's more useful than his old man. Sick note bloody Jones, the closest he usually got to coal was when he sat in front of the fire.'

His father was in good form today: nothing was left unsaid, which the old man thought healthy and honest, and never weak. Baldock stood by the window again, letting sunlight wash up against him. He watched his father slurp his tea, his thinning grey hair slicked back over his head in defiant vanity, watery blue eyes still active, and a scar marking his forehead like a blue vein. The TV was turned off.

'Waste of bloody time, all of it,' the old man said.

'Have you read the paper?'

'What for? And why are you stuck in the house all day?'

'I'm a carer, dad. That's what carers do.'

'Is that what they call you?'

It was true, he was a carer, and the state paid him for it, which amused Baldock. The old man was perfect cover, especially now things had got a little sticky with TJ. He should have seen that coming, the kid had always been the one most likely to break ranks, learning from him all the time, until he felt ready to branch out himself – on *his* territory. TJ had almost fouled up a smooth operation, and he knew too much.

His mobile rang. It was Tony.

'TJ's been seen, boss,' Tony said, 'he's raised his crappy head.'

'Where?'

'He's back with his mother. Rob saw him sneaking in the back way.'

'Okay.'

'You want the boys to do anything?'

'No, I'll sort it. Go on about your business.'

His father snorted.

'That a new toy? Isn't the phone downstairs enough for you?'

'Progress, dad.'

'Progress, be buggered. Now that's a slippery word if there ever was one.'

'Do you want me to get you one?'

'Now who the hell would I phone?'

Jesus on the main line might be good, Baldock thought.

'What are you grinning at?'

'Do you feel like going downstairs, Dad?'

'Nah, no point. Pass me that boxing book.'

It was a thick volume on long-gone fighters that his father had almost worn out with his shuffling fingers. It was the closest thing to a Bible he had.

'Look, I'm going out for a while,' Baldock said. 'You'll be all right?'

'Aye, go on, it will give me a bit of peace.'

Baldock was supposed to be a full time carer but often left his father, when business called, and it certainly called tonight. He remembered TJ's mother from school, a girl worn out with two kids by twenty, looking old at thirty, then trying to hang onto a series of disappearing men before she was forty. TJ had been her first kid.

Baldock locked his father in, it was the best way, and left their large end-terrace by the back door. He'd sit on the hillside for an hour, until the light faded. TJ wasn't going anywhere tonight.

There was a haze in the valley as the last of the sun went away, a yellow soft focus presentation of his world where sharp outlines congealed into hazy impressions. Baldock felt good but his father was right, time was passing, and forty would be the time to get out. The way the old man was, his caring might be over then, and he'd amassed enough money now. His operation had led a charmed life amidst the failures of many of his rivals because he had kept his head down and didn't flaunt it. Baldock had a certain reputation now, honed over the years, built on myth as much as substance: that was all that was needed in his kingdom of the lost.

Something swooped low overhead. The hawk hadn't expected him to be in the undergrowth and was startled when he sat up. It sped away from him, showing its undercarriage of lighter brown, which the fading light just caught. Baldock had always liked birds of prey. They led such short, savage lives. He remembered that time when he came across a shooter in the forestry, a man of his own age who he'd known slightly. When he saw Baldock coming he'd proudly held up the remains of a buzzard. Baldock knocked him down with one blow and kicked him hard a few times. As the man groaned, semi-conscious, unsure of what was happening, he'd smashed his airgun against a tree. I'll kill you next time, was all he said as he left the scene, feeling exhilarated and angry to his very core. He'd never heard anything back from the man.

Baldock got up and brushed himself down. It was well into dusk now, dark enough for him. He moved almost imperceptibly through the trees, his big frame diminished by years of practice.

Baldock entered TJ's estate from the hillside, well away from the main road. He hadn't been here for years, others ran his errands now. He skirted gardens cluttered with junk and rubbish, like adventure playgrounds for the insane. Baldock glanced back at the mountain to see a last smear of light strike the trees, and a last moment of green colour fade to black. He was struck by the difference just half a mile and people could make.

TJ's house was in a cul-de-sac, and it was particularly rancid. One window was boarded up, one marked by a shrivelled net curtain, and a kids' trike in need of wheels lay on the path. Baldock went to the back where he heard voices. One of them was TJ's. He stood by the kitchen door for a moment, tracing the conversation. TJ's mother wanted him gone but it was too late.

He kicked open the door. TJ was sitting at a small table, rolling a cigarette. His face drained of what little colour it had when he saw him.

'Baldock! Look, I can explain. You got it all wrong, man.'

As if she was programmed to do so, his mother started to scream, and shout, a hysterical combination which she though might have an effect on Baldock. She was wrong. As she stepped in front of her son TJ tried to get away but it was hopeless, Baldock caught him and flung him out into the garden.

'Relax,' Baldock told the mother, 'everything's cool. I'm not going to touch him, just get a few things straight. All you have to do is keep your mouth zipped.' He placed a roll of twenties onto the table. TJ's mother was torn between loyalty and need. Need won. She took the money and Baldock took TJ.

TJ whimpered as Baldock dragged him along, whining words coming from him as he was marched into the woods.

'Gimme something, Baldock,' TJ gasped. 'I gotta score. It's been three days now.'

'Yip. Three days of ducking and diving. Why did you come back here? I'm surprised even you could be that stupid.'

'Didn't have anywhere else to go, did I? Look, I'll work for nothing for you, I still got all the contacts.'

'Yeah, *my* contacts.'

Baldock pushed TJ in front of him and the boy made no attempt to get away. He staggered along like a rabbit petrified by light. The world Baldock operated in knew about TJ's treachery and any act of kindness now would be seen as weakness, and he wasn't known for that. He couldn't afford to be.

They walked up onto the hillside, Baldock stopping when they got to what locals called *The Crag*, a rocky outcrop that fell away to a twenty-foot drop.

'Where we going,' TJ asked, 'and why we stopping here?'

He sank to the ground, quieter now. He looked like something about to be preyed on, crouching, shivering, frozen with fear, and waiting for something to fall on him.

Baldock took two wraps from a pocket and stuffed them into one of TJ's. Gratitude flooded his victims' face, and for one crazy moment he felt joy before terror pushed it out again.

'There you are,' Baldock said, 'something for later, if you get to later.'

'Don' hurt me, Baldock, please don' hurt me.'

'I told your mother I wouldn't touch you and I always keep my word.'

He pulled an unconvinced TJ to his feet, and marched him to the edge of the crag.

'We'll call this a test of faith, TJ. Do you know what faith is?'

'I dunno what the fuck you talking about.'

'Faith in yourself. It's a beautiful thing, makes the world go round, you could say.'

They stood on the edge of the drop. Beneath them lay a carpet of fern and stunted trees.

'Jump when you're ready, TJ. Just pick your spot. I'm going to sit over here and enjoy the night.'

'For God's sake, Baldock, you crazy bastard.'

'I'm offering you a way back into the fold. Call it self-help. All you have to do is jump.'

TJ's face was the colour of the pale moon that was showing itself above the far mountain. It was a long few minutes and for the first time in ten years Baldock felt like a cigarette. In his early dealing days he'd often sat in dark and secret places, waiting and smoking, marked by the speck of red light that glowed off his cigarette. He'd broken his tobacco addiction, and had never had any other.

Maybe it was Baldock's sudden shift in position, maybe TJ

thought he was coming towards him with violent intent but TJ was gone, his cry taken by the wind as he fell. Baldock stood on the crag and searched for him in the ferns. TJ was there, moving slightly, a leg twisted under him. Baldock made his way down and quickly found the groaning TJ. They were not far from the mountain road and Baldock dragged TJ towards it, but not too roughly.

'You've done well, TJ,' he murmured, 'faith has pulled you through. Come and see me when you get out of hospital. No words now.'

Baldock phoned for an ambulance with his new mobile phone, and stood in the shadowed trees until it came. He heard TJ say that he'd lost his footing whilst out for a walk. No one asked why he was walking in the dark, it was best not to round these parts.

His father knocked on the floor as soon as Baldock opened the back door of their terrace. He went upstairs.

'Where you been? I'm not supposed to be left this long.'

'Went out for a bit of air.'

'One of your mystery trips, was it?'

The food on the tray had not been eaten.

'I've been thinking dad, how would you like a bit of sun? Might do your chest good.'

'What the hell are you talking about? You sound like you've been in the bloody sun too long.'

'Why not? We've got the wheelchair now. I was thinking maybe Normandy, you've always wanted to go back there. Weather will be good this time of the year, and we can afford it. I can take you anywhere you like.'

For once he'd surprised the old man.

'I was only eighteen when we landed on that beach,' his father said, 'it seems like a million years ago, and just yesterday somehow. I couldn't even swim. None of us could. Some boys drowned before they even set foot on land.'

Baldock rearranged the pillows and tidied the bed.

'There's a big fight coming up in Vegas, we could go on there afterwards. Now that place is really hot, and you could check out those lumbering bears in the flesh.'

'You're not in trouble here, are you?'

'Am I ever? Well, what do you think? It'll be our first family outing. Ever.'

'I'd have to get a passport.'

'I'll take that as a yes, then. We could go for a month or so.'

Baldock eased his father into a sleeping position, and gave him the last of his pills.

'You haven't been a bad son,' the old man murmured, 'all things considered. Your mother did her best to ruin you. She always wanted you for herself, and I was just there to provide the money. Do you know, I never thought Mary would go first, any more than she did. It's funny how things work out.'

Baldock took up his window position and tried to cast out doubts from his mind, the strange thoughts that gnawed at him from time to time. Terraces snaked along each side of the valley, uneven undulations soaked in orange streetlights. They were the lights of his world, and his world had become ordered again. It had been a good day.

A QUESTION OF BALANCE

It was a question of balance. Emrys knew that a few inches either way and the bike would topple over. Coffins were not usually transported like this: never in fact, especially in Cwmcrafu, but Em was not a very big man and it was not a very big coffin. Biodegradable cardboard did not weigh much.

Emrys attached the coffin to the rear of the seat, strapping it onto the metal plate there, where it stuck out on either side like an over-sized stabiliser. As he pushed the bike up gradients it fought against the straps, as if the box was already filled with an occupant not quite ready for it. Recklessly, a winded Em rode the bicycle down the hill, the strange cargo behind him spurring him on as he sped past the startled faces of old men and boys shouting out colourful encouragement. Flustered and red-faced, he offered them his upturned finger, which was a mistake.

He lost control of the bike and slid off the road into the brambled and permanently soggy ground that flanked it. He lay dazed for a while, head echoing with the taunts of the kids, and when his eyes cleared he saw shards of his coffin strewn around him. A pink condom lay inches from his nose, used and discarded the previous night. Perhaps it would have been better if he had stayed home.

Staying home was what Emrys Emilio Matthews did best. As a young man he had learnt this was his best policy, long since perfected into an art form. He had realised that life would always be too short for him, its days never long enough to serve his ideas and dreams, so he decided he wouldn't make the effort to realise any of them. It was inertia for him, and he became a great success at it. Most called him lazy, the epitome of it in fact, but he scoffed at them and their lives of wage bondage, and pointed out his exotic middle name, a whim of his father's.

Only one thing worried Em in life, and that was the terrible thought of another life after it, that the hoped for big sleep might turn out to be something else and he would have to go through it all again and maybe even have to work next time around. It was Marlowe who told him about the cardboard coffin.

'They put you in a small plot of ground somewhere and plant a tree over you for a few hundred quid,' Marlowe said. 'No religious mumbo-jumbo, no rip-off by wax-work smilers, be perfect for you.'

'Didn't you work for an undertaker once?' Em asked

'Aye, that guy down the valley. Only for six weeks though. *The inevitability of death is my life*, he used to say – creepy prat.'

Marlowe sized up Emrys as they lounged in the lounge of the 'Spite, enviously glancing at his flowing silver locks as he patted his own wispy oasis of hair.

'Christ, you look like a druid,' Marlowe said. 'Why don't you get it cut – a man of your age?'

'What for?'

Marlowe shrugged as they eked out their pints to record

23

lengths, even for them, until the remnants lay like stagnant, bitter pools at the bottom of their glasses.

'This place should be done up,' Marlowe muttered. 'Falling apart, it is.'

'Nonsense, you'll be asking for it to be cheerful next. Jenkins' sign above the front door is like a bible to me – *No Children! No Food! No Music!* The exclamation marks are a masterstroke. The man deserves a medal. He'd include *No Women!* too if he thought he could get away with it. What would *cheerful* be doing round here anyway? Around me? You have to be stupid *and* energetic to look on the bright side, that place where the grass is greener, etc etc.'

Jenkins the landlord approached, carving his way towards them by swiping at tables with his towel. No one else was in the lounge.

'Just about finished, boys? I'm calling time. Like you two called time on buying anything an hour ago.'

Jenkins wrung the towel in his beefy hands. He had the knack of smiling and sneering at the same time. They swallowed the last dregs of their ancient ale, winced, and handed him the glasses.

'Last of the big spenders,' Jenkins said, as he showed them his back.

They wandered home. Marlowe lived one street down from Emrys with his father, his ridiculously old, belligerently bed-ridden, still alive father. His wife had given up the ghost years ago. Emrys bade him good night. He regretted the fact that his one friend never read, and that the cinemas were closed down before he ever got round to going to them. Marlowe had managed a life free of knowledge and witticisms on his name would be lost on him. When they called him Marsh in school he was bemused, not angry.

The coffin was in the back yard, under a tarpaulin made out of bin-liners. Emrys sat by it for a while, musing on his last resting place. The box was still out of shape from the accident, but he had rebuilt it as best he could, mending its wounds with thick tape. It might disintegrate before I do, he thought.

There was almost a full moon out, casting a spectral glow on the yard. Emrys felt his two pints working on him. *Go on, get in the box, and try it out for size,* his tipsy inner voice coaxed. He opened the lid and probed around his last resting place, then went back inside the house for a pillow.

It was a mild spring night and the pillow made it much more comfortable. Emrys was able to stretch out and rest his head, as the moon worked its way across the sky, looking down on him like a giant yellow eye. He sighed and folded his arms after he pulled the lid in place, shutting out all but a corner of the moonlit night.

Sleep did not come easily in his new home. Emrys wasn't a good sleeper at the best of times, not enough was ever done in the day to tire out his thoughts, and they always sprang into life with fresh, nocturnal possibilities.

The Dawes cat jumped up onto the lid, he could see it through the thin opening he had left, its inquisitive, translucent eyes shining in the pale light. Emrys coughed and the startled cat scuttled away. He folded his arms again and relaxed. He rather liked the position. Old people should have a lot to look back on, I have only a lifetime of easy-paced thinking, he mused, but this thought soothed him and sleep eventually came.

Jared Dawes was nosy; it was nosiness honed over six decades, now flowering to perfection in the garden of his retirement, and given full rein with the demise of his wife. Emrys's coffin intrigued and infuriated him. It was such a source of gossip in the village, but his neighbour said nothing to *him* about it. *My end is mine own*, was all Emrys would mouth, grinning slyly. Jared hated that man of few words, any man of few words.

Its tarpaulin removed, the coffin proudly showed itself to the bright morning sunshine. Even the village looked good in such light. It's just a glorified cardboard box, Dawes muttered to himself, as he looked out of his window, wishing the wife was still around to see this. Wishing the kids would call to see him more often, or even at all.

Perhaps the cover had blown off. He could tell Emrys, maybe even get the old fool talking. Dawes called over the wall, knowing that Emrys was an early riser. There was no answer. Maybe he was already out, though the 'Spite wouldn't be open for hours yet. The coffin-clad yard was tempting. Just a quick look in the box to see if it had a lining, that's all.

The back gate yielded to Jared's thrust, rotten wood disintegrating in his hands. He scanned his neighbour's unwashed windows, then cupped his hands and peered into the kitchen. He saw just the remnants of a loaf on the table and a few books strewn around. Emrys kept those everywhere.

Dawes wondered where the man could have gone so

early. He wanted to know, but the enticing box might provide adequate compensation. He approached it, and walked round it a few times watched by the cat on the wall. That bugger always seemed to know *something*, a sullen knowledge was in its eyes, taunted him. Dawes hated it as much as his wife had loved it.

There was a noise from the coffin. Dawes jumped a little and hesitantly approached it. He heard the noise again. Stronger this time, almost human. Damn it, his ears were playing up. As if his ticker wasn't enough. The coffin moved. *It bloody moved.* The lid slid off. Something inside pushed it off. Pain clutched at Dawes's chest and he fell back against the wall. The cat made itself scarce with a yowl. Bloody hell, Jared gasped, as Em sat up, smiled, and began to rub the sleep from his eyes.

'What are you doing there, Dawes?' Emrys asked. 'What time is it?'

Jared Dawes did not answer. He sat down heavily, eyes blinking against the pain, unable to do anything but gasp. Wiping sleep from his eyes, Emrys did not quite grasp the situation until his neighbour was dead, quickly, and with the minimum of fuss.

Emrys emerged from the coffin to examine Dawes. Thoughts of resuscitation procedures ambled through his mind, but did not stay there. It would have meant too much effort without reward.

Seeing that his neighbour's back door was open Emrys went in and used his phone. By the time the ambulance came Dawes was neatly laid out on the yard floor and the coffin re-tarpaulined. It was the most work he had ever done of a morning, and it was more hard graft fielding the questions of the police. He needed the drink Marlowe suggested later.

'Maybe that box is jinxed,' Marlowe said.

'Nonsense. Dawes should have kept his nose out.'

'Didn't the police think it strange though, you sleeping out – in that?'

'Well, I suppose it was a novel form of camping,' Emrys said, with some pride.

'It hasn't put you off this stuff then?'

'Not at all. The box and me are settled in now. No, Dawes just hastened his time, that's all. You could say he played at Pandora.'

'Eh?'

'Pandora.'

Marlow thought for a moment. 'You mean Pandora's People, that leggy lot from the seventies? What have they—?'

'Never mind, Marsh. Count out this loose change. See if we can make another pint.'

There was enough for one pint and one half. Emrys let Marlowe have the pint. He felt generous, and at one with the world.

FIREBUG

Before the fire my one small act of rebellion was to ignore a ringing telephone. I enjoyed the heady guilt that came with it. It was a small, rather empty victory over Mr Swirmley, a man I thought had eyes all over his body, and able to see through walls.

I had worked for him for seventeen years, since leaving school. He had snapped me up with my two O-levels and kept me to him ever since. The Picture Box had been shaky even then, forever on the brink of closure as its public moved away to feed off free images in their front rooms. We relied on a scattering of pensioners, children, and the occasional groping couple. These, and Swirmley's extreme care with money, just about kept us going.

I started on a thin wage which never did take on much weight, but I stayed at the 'Box, for the films. Films were all I had ever been interested. I inhabited the worlds of old classics and drew comfort from their safe, unreal worlds. It was a kind of life, for me.

At the 'Box I was projectionist, handyman, cleaner, and film collector. There was just the cashier, the part time usherette and myself. But in the projection booth I was alone, and in control. The equipment was old and needed constant watching over, but the old man before me had been patient in his tuition and I was master of every vicious whim of the reels.

Swirmley seemed ageless. There was an air of decay about the man, but it never got any worse. He had been bald when I first met him, with a few silver wisps of hair sticking out at either side of his head. They used to gleam when his pate was caught in the projection beam, and his suit was always the same. It was a blue chalk stripe, shiny with wear, and pockets bulging. A hearing aid cord dangled from his left ear, and trailed to his waistcoat pocket where the power pack was. It was old fashioned even then, like everything else in the 'Box it was decrepit, prone to letting out errant shrieks when the place was quiet. There were more modern and less obtrusive devices available, but Swirmley would not countenance the expense. The Picture Box tottered from crisis to crisis. Things got so bad we might have gone under, but Swirmley came up with an idea, and it changed my life forever.

We specialised in showing films a few months after the main circuit, padded out with *festivals* of old ones acquired on the cheap. These were my films, the stuff of my dreams, of everyone's dreams, once. Joan the cashier told how the 'Box would be packed with eager people in the old days, and more waiting outside, despite the presence of three other cinemas in the town. They came for the outsized images and outsized lives on the screen, colourful, wealthy lives they could inhabit for a few hours and live inside their fantasies. But that was before television, that herald of a softer age I somehow felt was a harder age.

'Sex, Eric, it's our only hope,' Swirmley said, 'S.E.X sex.'

He had called me into his office on a Friday afternoon. It

was high summer and the 'Box had settled into its seasonal emptiness. Even pensioners had better things to do.

'Sex, Mr. Swirmley?' I asked, feeling my face go red.

'Aye, some films are full of it. This is the seventies, Eric. We've had the swinging sixties, now we need something to follow them up, something to cheer people up with all this political stuff going on. Look, I've been going through the catalogues. Some of these films are dead cheap to hire. Foreign mind, but folks won't care about that, not when they know what's in 'em.'

I adjusted my glasses and flicked back a stray strand of hair, which I always did in times of stress. Swirmley circled his desk, looking like a self-satisfied fox with a chicken in its mouth. I dwindled in my chair, my skinny frame awkward, and my glasses steaming up.

'Do you think that's wise, Mr. Swirmley?' I managed to say.

'We don't have much choice, young man, not if we want to stay open.'

He placed a hand on my shoulder and pressed down hard. I knew this was a command.

I left the office in a daze and took refuge in my booth, where I fingered the last reel of Gone With The Wind. We showed it every August.

It took Swirmley a month to realise his plans. He disappeared for several days, and returned with a van full of stock.

'Soft core porn, they call this lot,' he said, 'German stuff mostly, but they have subtitles.'

'Won't we be showing anything else? What about our *Classics Week?*'

'It's not wanted any more. Not needed. Look, you want to keep your job, don't you?'

Swirmley started the sex on the first weekend of August. He gambled on a half page spread in the local paper, prompting an excited call from Harrison, the editor. Swirmley was nothing if not a showman. He knew there would be a sanctimonious leader in next week's edition, and that the land of the twitching net curtains would get fired up. It would be great publicity, and free, Swirmley's second favourite four letter word.

A rainy Saturday ensured we were full. Back were the rowdy youths and old men, and other people we had not seen in years, and couples, giggling and self-conscious. Solitary figures slipped in modestly, to secrete themselves on the ends of rows. Swirmley adorned the foyer, fat fingers in his waistcoat, eyes aglow with the head count. His glee, my shame.

Swirmley knew his town. There were complaints, but when local dignitaries threatened a ban, more people came. At first I tried not to look at the films, focusing mechanically and concentrating on the machines, but gradually, inexorably, I watched, as if the celluloid was pulling my eyes onto it. They were the first naked women I had ever seen, large breasted, with china-doll hair. It was quite unnerving. Suddenly Father Patrick was with me. I could hear his shouting words of hell and damnation, and feel his fists about to strike.

As I passed people on my way home I tried to melt into shop doorways, but at least it was dark. No matter what time of year, it was always dark when I went home. I entered our house quietly, knowing that mother would have retired. God knows what she was thinking.

By the middle of September, when the novelty of Swirmley's idea was waning, he deposited two canisters of film on my table.

'These will keeps things cooking nicely,' he said. 'We don't want the punters slacking off. They're calling this place the Sex Box now.'

I looked at the canisters. One said, *A Study of Sex, The Danish Way.*

'Right steamy stuff this is,' Swirmley said. 'Shows the lot it does, and we'll get away with it too because it's supposed to be educational.'

'Is it very... um... strong?'

'I just said, it's the real thing. And if the council pokes its snout in, we'll give 'em a private showing. They'll lap that up, two-faced bastards.'

It was the last straw. I went home that night with a decision made, my legs pumping out an uneven rhythm on the pavement, my lame leg hardly bothering me. I walked tall, for the first time in my life.

After a council debate, when the 'Box even featured on local television, the film was passed. On the first night there were queues around the block. This film was better quality stock and I was able to focus pin-sharp on its writhing contours. I saw the acts never mentioned in my family and watched like a prisoner, ashamed but trapped.

I waited and sweated all through that week until late Saturday night, but drunks still swirled around the town centre. It was past midnight when I was sure I could re-enter the cinema unobserved. I unlocked the side door and used the back stairs, the can of petrol heavy in my hand. The booth was the best place for the fire to start. It was the heart of my contaminated world, and the seat of my connivance.

I sloshed the petrol around, sickened by the smell. A trail of fuel led all the way down to the first seats. I put the empty can in a large film bag and added the two canisters of Danish film, without knowing why. Standing well back I threw a lighted rag into the booth. Flames immediately leapt up with a whoosh, and I ran back to the side entrance, feeling like I was in a scene witnessed in so many films. When the fire had reached the seats I went outside, re-locked the door and walked down the aide alley into the street with as much nonchalance as I could muster.

By the time I had climbed the hill to our house flames were shooting up high over the 'Box. I heard shouting, and the sirens of fire engines. They would not save it. The Picture Box was too ripe to be saved.

Swirmley phoned me at three in the morning.

'It's gone, Eric, it's all bloody gone.'

'What is. Mr. Swirmley? I don't understand.'

'The Box. Burnt to the bloody ground it is. And the café next door. I thought old man Galeozzi was going to have a fit when he told me.'

I regretted the loss of the café, but I knew Eddy and his family lived elsewhere.

'But how? I asked, 'how could it happen? I always double check everything before I close up.'

'I know you do, lad. It must have been an electrical fault, you know the state the place was in. I've got to prepare the insurance stuff now. Thank God we were doing so well, or they might say we burnt the place down ourselves. A lot of that goes on these days.'

'Yes, Mr. Swirmley.'

He softened his tone.

'Look Eric, you've been with me a long time, but you know what this means, don't you? Your job's gone for a Burton, Maude's too.'

'Yes, I see that.'

'When the insurance comes through I'll sort out a month's wages for you, and they might want a projectionist somewhere else, you never know.'

I did know. Projectionists were a dying breed. We were all heading for extinction.

'Yes, Mr. Swirmley. Thank you.'

Next morning I hummed a tune from one of the shows as I prepared mother's tea. As I took it up to her each creak of the stairs was a welcome friend. I put the tray down by the bed and gently tapped her shoulder.

In my own room the early sun streamed through the blinds, carving up the room with patterns of light. I stood at the window and looked down on the blackened shell of the Picture Box. I did not feel as bad as I thought I would. Sex lay in canisters under the floorboards, to act as a memorial to my action. I felt such pride, I felt it surge through me like an electric charge. Just like in a film.

JOHN LONEWOLF HAWKINS

A bug swirled around in the tub, spiralling towards the drain hole in its own miniature whirlpool. John watched its struggles as he towelled himself dry. He thought it had drowned already, but as the last of the water ran out it lay awash on the brass bar that crossed the hole, then stirred. Whisker-like feet tried in vain to get a purchase on the slippery surface. John thought of ending its struggle by flicking it down into the abyss, but he picked it up gently between thumb and forefinger and placed it on a window ledge. The desert air quickly dried it out and the bug trundled away to safety. Each spring Hairy Marys came into the house, and each spring they fell into the tub.

In the bedroom Lena stirred, her siesta over. She called out a greeting that John answered. He went to her. Lena sat at the old dresser, her face caught by slanting light and the yellowed oak of the wood. For him she was ageless. The light etched her high cheekbones and put a shine to the ebony of her eyes. John watched her brush her hair. He'd always watched Lena brush her hair. It was still a young girl's hair, even if its black was shot through with silver now. Rich life fizzed from it as the hard brush connected.

John moved past Lena to the kitchen, where coffee was heating on the stove. He poured out two cups and went out onto the porch. The heat had diminished but the skyline still danced with the land, two sun-drunk loons merging together. Lena joined him, sitting on the rocker and humming gently an old song.

'So, Dan will soon be home,' Lena said.

John grunted but did not answer. He preferred to watch the sun fall in silence, in the custom of his people. He was Navajo, mixed with a touch of Mescalero. He was proud of the latter, his throwback to a wild, proud past, out of keeping with the farming and trading ways of the Navajo. The agency man had allotted the name Hawkins to his grandfather, back in the old days.

John was sixty-four, with a nose splayed flat, widely spaced eyes, and dark copper skin grooved and pummelled by a lifetime in the sun. He had kept his hair short since his army days. He did not live on tribal lands any more, but his identity was imprinted on him in early childhood and still flowered in old age. He was of the last generation to be brought up in lodges, and sitting on the porch at sunset, his thoughts were often back there, amongst the tales and smells of his grandparents' world. He still saw them clearly, their creased faces like monuments, their eyes distant with ancient freedom.

Two years ago John had driven his last load across the desert he loved, covering in a day what would have been six months roaming space for the tribes. Trucking for a frozen food company, the only job on offer after the army.

'Lost in your thoughts again,' Lena said. 'I swear one day your face is going to turn to stone.'

'There's not much else to do right now.'

'Dan will be here tomorrow. You still haven't finished his room.'

John stood in the centre of Dan's bedroom. It was like any other abandoned by a college kid. A few trophies, team pennants, rock posters, a miniature plastic skeleton hanging by a string. The bits and pieces kids pick up and leave.

There was one wall left to paint. He played the brush up and down, turning faded yellow into bright white, like the light at sun-up. Dan did not get home much but this time he was bringing a girl with him, Rachel, who he said he was going to marry. They had never even met her.

John finished the painting and cleared up his stuff. It was time to get out into the desert, where he could think. Dan always mixed him up, and now pride mingled with a sense of loss.

John started up the old pick-up with Lena's clucking disapproval in his ears. Five minutes of due west highway and the town was forgotten, another five minutes and he was on a dirt road where man was gone and the land unchanged. No one wanted the desert much, apart from the military. It held nothing that could easily be turned into money. His nostrils quivered as they fine-tuned to the air, which was sharp, and smelling of space and old heat as the desert began to chill and dry out the sweat on his back.

John stopped the pick-up on his usual ridge, where he could look down on the burnt gold plain spreading out in front of him like waves of a sea. Lizards nearby snatched the last heat from the rocks before scuttling back to their holes. Even they had a place here that was right for them.

It seemed that the Mojave had gathered up in a vortex of heat and air all that John loved about it. He smelt the arrowhead clumped around acacia trees, and the creosote as old wood cracked. Green mesquite shimmered in front of him and bright orange nolina flowers caught the sun, their dagger-like leaves moving softly in the light breeze.

He wandered around for a while, until the sun went down, which happened quickly here. There was a sense of shadow, then darkness. John felt better. This place could always be relied on to calm him.

Later that night John and Lena ate supper on the porch, John piling food into his mouth rapidly, something Lena had never been able to get him to change.

'You spend too much time out there,' Lena said, 'it's a lonesome place.'

Her eyes were reproachful but she knew how strongly the old ways pulled on her man, especially now that he had time to indulge them. She felt left out sometimes, pushed to the edge of his thoughts.

Dan Hawkins arrived next morning. He'd driven overnight to avoid the heat and stood on the porch as breakfast was being prepared. Tall and spare, he was not much like his father at first glance, but the stubborn look was there, and sometimes he flashed the same hawkish glare. Rachel was also tall, looking down on Lena as she entered the house. She was blond and fresh. Lena hugged her son and John waved an awkward hand towards him, and took the one Rachel offered him.

'I'm glad to meet you at last, Mr. Hawkins. It's a delightful house.'

'We like it,' John answered.

They sat at the table and ate breakfast. Dan didn't say much but looked for signs of approval from his parents. Lena's was forthcoming.

'We got your letter about the internship,' Lena said. 'We're real proud.'

'Yeah, it's a stroke of luck,' Dan said. 'Lots of guys were after it.'

'Luck had nothing to do with it,' Rachel said. 'Dan was the best man for the job.'

John watched the talkers, slyly through his brows, something he had perfected when he first mixed with white people. Dan's woman was pretty much what he had expected and she came into the house as if she had always belonged.

Dan took Rachel out into the desert after breakfast, in the red sports car her father had given her. Lena waved them away and John was glad they would not be able to leave the main road, not in a car like that.

'She's real nice,' Lena said.

'Yip.'

'I know what you're thinking, sour man,' Lena muttered. 'You can't choose for him, John. Not his woman, not anything. You ought to be proud of him, doing so well. A doctor, one of our people a doctor, and you worked all the hours to pay for it. And Rachel wants him, even if we are poor. That should count for something.'

'I guess.'

John settled into the rocker, making it sing out its song of tired springs. He knew that his short answers infuriated Lena. He heard her clearing the table, singing as she worked, then she cut a few flowers from the patch at the rear of the house. They smelt of the morning air and would make splashes of orange and red against the white walls of Dan's bedroom.

It was two days before John spent some time alone with his son. They drank in a bar that not so many years ago would not serve *Indians*. He'd always hated the word, and the irony of its inaccuracy.

'Want to know what I think of her, huh?' John said.

'Sure. Mom likes Rachel. How about you, dad?'

'I don't know her, and I'm a cautious man, you know that.'

'Mom's told me how you're out in the desert all hours.'

'Right.'

'What are you looking for there, the old ways? Jesus, do you have to wallow in the past? It's not fair on Mom. *I* want to be part of the real world.'

Dan finished his bourbon and chased it down with beer. Anger flushed the dark hue of his face, anger John liked.

'Would you prefer I wear buckskin and live in a canyon somewhere?' Dan continued. 'Did you? No, you drove a white man's truck in a white man's world. You had no choice, same as me.'

Dan lowered his voice as a few men glanced over at them.

John grinned at his son. 'They'll think you're going on the warpath,' he said.

'That's almost a joke for you. Look, I'm grateful for what

you've given me, but now I want to be a success. A success at my job. Can't you be glad for me?'

John wanted to say that he was, but the words twisted on his tongue. He reached out a hand and tapped Dan on the shoulder.

'Medicine men were pretty important to the old tribes. Can you make it rain?'

Dan smiled and raised his glass.

They finished their drinks and drove home in the pick-up, evening light turning from red to purple on the dashboard. John saw Dan as a baby in Lena's arms, the only one that came to them. He had been nearly forty when the boy was born. Too old, maybe, too firmly set in his ways, definitely.

Dan went into town on business the next day, leaving Rachel in the house. John padded around nervously, evading her attempts to draw him into conversation. The desert beckoned him and he saw the reprimand already forming in Lena's face. She was right. It was his escape. Just like the lizards he too needed a bolt hole.

'If you're going out there why don't you take Rachel,' Lena said, pitching her voice so that their guest could hear.

Rachel walked with him to the pick-up, a little excited, her teeth catching the sun and flashing white signals back in perfect symmetry. John licked his tongue over the remnants of his own teeth and set his jaw.

They shared the single long seat of the truck, a worn brown plastic which let in all the bumps of the road.

'You've had this truck a long time,' Rachel said.

'No point changing. It still runs.'

Rachel did not try to break the silence again. John

screwed up his eyes against the sun. A lifetime of doing so had given the skin around his eyes the texture of old walnuts. Rachel hid from the glare behind her Raybans.

He stopped the truck on a rise, but it was not his usual spot. They looked down on a plain of variegated yellow, red and brown, sifted by heat haze, so that its true contours could only be guessed at. It was a place of twisted branch and rock, but of stubborn life, too, if you knew where to look for it. There was no noise and only vultures moved, far off in the sky, drifting on thermals in high circles, watching.

'Something's dead or dying out there,' John muttered, nodding his head in the direction of the birds.

'I've never seen them before, except in movies.'

'Guess they look the same as them movie birds.'

Rachel laughed at this and took it as a cue.

'You don't like me much, do you?' she asked.

John resisted the urge to shrug his shoulders.

'Dan's told me how you feel about the past,' Rachel continued. 'Is it something to do with that? Or is it my colour? My bank balance? I'm not ashamed of who I am, any more than you are, and I don't overdose on pride either.'

John noticed new colour in Rachel's face. Twin lances of red marked her cheeks. He clenched the steering wheel and didn't respond for a while. A vague pain ran up his arm, something he had noticed a few times before.

'You've spoken straight with me,' John said. 'I didn't think you would, but don't try to get inside my head, not even Lena can do that. And don't take me personally, either.'

John got out of the truck and stood on the rise, sifting the earth with his boots. Rachel joined him.

'It *is* beautiful,' she said.

'You ever handle a pick-up?' John asked. 'I want to walk back.'

'It's too far.'

'Nah, I do it all the time.'

'I don't know, John.'

'Get on back now. Tell Lena I'll be back by supper time. The truck is old but she's well behaved. Not like me.'

'Okay. If that's what you really want.'

Rachel turned to go but John stopped her with a hand.

'Maybe we made a start today,' he murmured.

As he walked John felt life pulse all around him. It was inside him. The dirt road he trudged did not mark the desert much, man was not lord here and never would be, and people were still as rare as water. He covered the ground in steady strides, chanting softly to himself. Lena would go nuts when he got home. He smiled at the thought of his wife animated and fire-eyed. She had put up with a lot over the years. Maybe he *could* change a little, even now.

John walked a few miles, rounded a bend and saw the pick-up slewed over on its side, its wheels sunk in soft sand. He jogged towards it. Rachel was trapped inside, her body pushed against the passenger door. The window was jammed, but he managed to stretch a hand through a gap to tap her shoulder. She moaned as she came round.

'I hit a rock and rolled over,' she gasped. 'I guess I was going too fast.'

'Can you move? Have you broken anything?'

She moved gingerly, and shook her head.

'No, I don't think so. I must have passed out though.'

'There's a bump on your forehead. You must have hit the screen.'

He tried to open the driver's door but the lock had jammed. The other door was flush against the sand. John knew this was his fault.

'Hang on, I'll try to right the truck.'

John tried to push the pick-up back onto four wheels, his face shining as he heaved against the weight. He moved it a few inches out of the sand, but the weight was too much. There was pain in his chest, like a pent up fist trying to open. He sat down heavily. It was a lot of pain.

'You look worse than I feel,' Rachel said.

'I'll try again when I get my breath.'

'No, don't. If you can smash the front screen I think I can climb out.'

'Okay. Cover your face then, with the blanket in the back.'

John found a heavy rock and pounded the glass until it shattered. He cleaned it out and took hold of Rachel's shirt. After more effort he managed to pull her free. She was bruised about the face but otherwise all right. There was more pain. Arrows fired into his chest. John sat down heavily and bit his lip.

'You shouldn't have tried to push the truck,' Rachel said, squeezing his arm.

John smiled through clenched teeth, and the sky was a crazy, blue ceiling dancing above him. He knew the vultures were for him. Pain seared up again, then became distant, almost a memory as he took in the last of his desert. Rachel was calling to him but it was a faint, far-off voice, like an echo in the mountains. A rushing came to his ears, a flapping of wings.

Six weeks later Lena saw John's memorial stone put in place, in the small cemetery on the edge of town, at the start of the desert. His body was not there. With Dan she had scattered his ashes along the ridge he loved and watched the wind take him. From Rachel she knew of John's last minutes, her silent man making an effort to come to terms with a big change in his life,

Lena placed flowers from her garden around the stone, casting a small arc of colour over his name. They would shrivel quickly in the sun but she'd replace them every time.

NOTHING HAPPENS

I met, or rather discovered, Madame Amelier by chance. She was sitting in the corner of a bar, which was otherwise empty. There was a bottle of Ricard on her table, and a black and gold box of Black Sobranie cigarettes alongside it. I hadn't seen them in years.

The woman was smoking one, in an elegant gold holder. She held it like a prop against her bright red lips, far too red for a woman of her age, which I guessed to be about seventy. She was dressed quietly, in contrast to the garish slash of her mouth, just a simple black jacket, and something almost colourless beneath. Her legs, what I could see of them, were still shapely. Neat, that was the word I was looking for, this was a neat woman, almost bird-like. Audrey Hepburn came to mind, how she might have looked if she'd lived to this age. It was early for Ricard.

August had been hot, hot to the point of madness. The paper under my arm told of the many deaths the heat had caused, old people for the most part, dying alone in their airless apartments. I needed something cold, and the Bar de la Croix was the first watering hole I saw. It wasn't my kind of place at all, filled as it was with heavy mahogany furnishings that spoke of another age. Even worse was the stuffed raven on the bar. I felt there was still life in those intense glass eyes. But the bar was cool, wonderfully cool.

I nodded to the woman as a small man appeared from the back room, too well dressed for this time of the day, but right for here. He bade me *bonjour* and I ordered a Perrier, which he treated with the reverence of fine wine, pouring it out into a long glass full of ice and lemon. I would have expected no less. I noticed there were no tables or chairs outside the bar, which was very rare for Paris. As I looked around the old woman beckoned to me.

'Why don't you sit here, monsieur, with me?'

For an insane moment I wondered if she might be the oldest working girl in town, but put this down to the heat. I smiled, and did sit down at her table.

'It is so hot outside,' she said, or rather breathed, for her mouth hardly moved or disturbed the gold holder. 'It passed forty yesterday. A record, they say.'

I murmured assent, feeling awkward being so close to her, for the round table was too small, and too intimate. A delicate fragrance was about her, something flowery I didn't recognise.

'We don't usually open so early,' the old woman said, 'but it takes one's mind off this weather – isn't that right, Albert?'

'Certainly, Madame.'

So this was her place, but it did not seem right for her, especially its name. Too heavy, too much like the stuff in the bone yard across the road, and Madame did not strike me as the religious type.

'I don't think I've seen you in Montparnasse before,

monsieur. Have you come to look for someone – over there? So many do.'

She gestured, almost imperceptibly with her head, towards the cemetery gates.

'Not really,' I said.

'But it will be cooler there, no matter what the weather, it is always cooler there.' She glanced at me, her eyes moving up and down my long frame. 'You look like a man who reads. Are you?'

I nodded hesitantly.

'Well, you'll find Sartre, and Beauvoir, over there, next door to each other in death, as they were in life. Theirs are rather small graves amongst the grand tombstones.'

'Perhaps they are making a statement,' I said.

'Yes, perhaps so.'

She took a final long drag on her cigarette, exhaling smoke in a thin line that curled upwards to the ceiling like a blue-grey snake. 'I met Simone a few times, in the old days.'

'Really?'

Madame lit another cigarette.

'Do you mind?'

'Not at all.'

She did not elaborate about De Beauvoir. Somehow, I would have been disappointed if she had. My eyes were accustomed to the gloom of the bar now, and I saw the dog for the first time. It gave me a start. In a basket at her side of the table, almost under her feet, lay something small, and as black as the raven. It looked at me like the raven had too, only this time the eyes moved.

'This is Mimi,' she said, poking the dog gently with her foot. 'She's my best friend and confidant.'

Madame held out a child-sized hand, bare of rings, which I took. It was warm and moist, without any grip whatsoever, and it fell through my hand like water. I said my own name. I thought she'd remark on it and the accent of my French but she said nothing, and for a while we sat in silence. I felt obliged to stay, at least until my glass was empty.

'English?' she asked, after her cigarette was finished.

I said no, and expected the usual geographic run-around but none came. This woman seemed curious in very small doses. I sensed her quizzical air of amusement, but her sadness more. I looked again at her bare hands. A woman of her age and demeanour should have signs of life past, rings of testimony, triumph, and loss. For a moment I thought of my own.

'Would you like a glass of my Ricard, monsieur? It is too tragic to drink alone.'

Before I could answer fingers snapped, and Albert appeared with another glass and a jug of iced water with lemon slivers floating in it. As I poured some out I could not prevent a smile and wondered how rare customers were in the Bar de la Croix.

'You remind me of my son,' my host said, and Albert muttered agreement as he made his way back to the bar. There was something wrong with his leg, and he shuffled across the wooden floor. 'I haven't seen him in years.'

It was my turn to be incurious.

Having checked me out, Mimi closed her eyes again. It was too much of an effort for her to keep them open. I knew how she felt. Last night's wine was punishing me. There was an insistent throb over an eye, and the headache was getting worse, yet I still drank the Ricard, enjoying the small clouds it made when mixed with the water. The greatest challenge for an alcoholic is not reaching for that first drink, and I did not feel like challenges this day. Maybe it was the hypnotic, stifling feel of the bar, and its strange inhabitants.

'I haven't seen his father either,' Madame continued, 'not for thirty-five years. Not since Charles was two.'

'Almost three,' Albert murmured from the bar.

'I couldn't hold him here, you see, monsieur.'

I nodded, feeling the first signs of anxiety. I might be stuck here for some time, trapped on an old woman's meanderings, and propped up with free Ricard. That was double jeopardy indeed.

'Pierre was a wanderer, and a dreamer, and he'd always revel in all the fine things he would never do, all the fine places he'd never go, as life passed him by. We had not the money, monsieur. Not then.'

She looked at me more closely.

'Hmm, you look like him too. I had a small shock when you came in, with the light behind you, in silhouette. So many years ran away from me. I had to look at my hands to remember my age. Foolish woman.'

The Ricard began to hit home, in that sly way it always did, and I was sweating again. I thought what Madame was saying was ironic. If life has passed anywhere by, it was this bar. I should have made my excuses and left, mingling with the Sunday flower bringers and inquisitive tourists over the road to ease my head. Madame Amelier read me.

'Don't be concerned, monsieur. You are not dealing with a mad woman. It's just that today is the birthday of my boy. He was born here, whilst his father was at the races. Please don't think I always drink Ricard at this time of the day.'

I smiled and nodded and hoped she did not notice my hand trembling on my glass. Of course she noticed. Drunks were her stock in trade. Her own grip was immobile, in keeping with the surroundings.

'You don't see your son?' I finally asked.

My question drew me further into her story, as I knew it would. Albert stopped polished his already gleaming bar and sat down at the table next to us, muttering to himself. I felt that, for some reason, each of them craved my captive audience.

'He does so well,' Madame said. 'In London. Something to do with finance, banks, that sort of thing. Albert reads me something about him from time to time in the newspapers. He does well, doesn't he, Albert?'

'*Bien sur*, Madame. He is what you call an *entrepreneur*, monsieur – a French word that is well travelled.'

Albert sighed, and looked at his hands.

It was a word that usually meant *charlatan* in my book, and it seemed a million miles away from Le Bar de la Croix. Madame had not answered my question. I examined her more closely, as discreetly as I could. She'd been a beauty, no doubt about that. Traces of it still remained, her fine bone structure was not that diminished by age and her hands were free of any arthritic mis-shaping.

Madame's green eyes watched me slyly. Was it her fault that she'd been abandoned twice over? Was she even telling the truth, and did I care? Too many questions for my headache but the Ricard was freeing up my mood. Besides, I had nothing better to do.

Nothing better to do. I'd had nothing better to do for the whole sweltering summer. When Paris had emptied in early August I had felt this keenly, something akin to loneliness that I tried to pass off as solitude.

'Coffee, monsieur? Albert asked. 'Espresso goes well with Ricard.'

I accepted the offer and wondered whether to reiterate my question but there was no need.

'Charles became his father,' Madame said. 'Perhaps it was inevitable, looking so like him. Looks are all in this world, everything else comes a poor second, don't you think?'

I shrugged as she went on.

'Yet there is always a price to pay. I was his, and his heart hardened as he grew up.'

'Madame,' Albert said softly from the bar, 'you did all a mother could do. All a wife could.'

Albert brought the coffee in a white and gold cup on a delicate blue saucer.

'Do you want something to eat, monsieur?' Madame asked. 'Some breakfast, perhaps? It's still early, after all. My treat, for your company.'

I declined, but the espresso was good and it kick-started my system again. Often I needed more than one attempt in the morning. A man stopped at the bar entrance, and we all looked up in expectation, as light shafted the doorway and cut the dust that mingled there. The man changed his mind and walked on.

'They often walk on now,' Madame murmured, but I felt she was glad we were not disturbed. As sunlight tried to penetrate the gloom I looked more closely at the drinks behind the bar. Nothing looked fresh. There were quarter full bottles of Pernod and Smirnoff, and whiskies I hadn't seen for years. This was a parade of old friends.

Madame poured herself another liberal measure of drink.

'Isn't it wonderful how it mingles with the water,' she muttered, 'like someone blowing smoke into the glass.'

Maybe I was with a fellow drunk here; usually only people like me studied booze like this, but her hands were much steadier than mine. I was getting gently tipsy, comfortable in the shadowy presence of my hosts. The headache lessened as my body welcomed its medicine. Albert sat with one hand in his black waistcoat, the other moving almost imperceptibly on the table. His fingers shuffled in the same way that his feet did. Madame stared at the entrance as if willing others to come in, smoking a third Sobranie, expertly loaded into her holder. I might have slipped into a doze if she had not spoken.

'I wonder what Charles is doing for his birthday,' she murmured. 'Maybe he is married now, I wouldn't know. I might even be a grandparent, monsieur.'

'Surely there is some way you can get in touch, maybe through his work – his friends?'

'Albert tried a few years ago, but got nowhere.'

The Ricard bottle was empty. Two sets of eyes alighted on it, a mutual hunger.

'Albert,' Madame said, flicking her cigarette towards the bottle, firmly enough for a few speck of its ash to break free.

Albert stood up slowly and stood behind her for a moment. He wanted to catch my attention, and pointed very deftly to his head, shaking a bony finger. Did he mean she'd had enough, or that she was mad, or both? Whatever he meant, Albert did as he was told. He went to the bar and brought another bottle of Ricard. Any more for me would make this a very long day. I let Madame pour some out for me and hoped she wouldn't notice if I did no more than touch the glass with my lips.

'I remember when Charles first went to school,' Madame continued. 'Taking him, trying to hide my concern, knowing that he'd be the only boy there who had never seen his father. What do they call them now, single-parent families? They were a rarity then, monsieur. I wondered how he'd be treated by the other boys.'

Her voice trailed off into an uncomfortable silence. She seemed to have the habit of doing this, cutting off information by a retreat into some other place. I needed the washroom and excused myself. Nothing had much changed in there since the place had been built. There was a porcelain urinal, and an oversized basin with large brass taps. There wasn't even a mirror but I knew my face would be puffy and red, and the smudges under my eyes increasingly dark. Today the Ricard would add to them. This was the face of a roué, Madame might think, and she wouldn't be far wrong. To cool myself, I dashed some water into it, splattering dark spots onto my white shirt.

As I re-entered the bar Albert pulled at my arm. I hadn't noticed him lurking in the shadows.

'Thank you, monsieur,' he whispered, 'for spending some time with Madame. With my wife.'

If he'd expected surprise on my part he got it.

'I was afraid no one would come in at all. The bar does not really function now, but Madame insisted we open today, and I thought it wise that we did. You have made it real, monsieur.'

'You don't behave like her husband,' I murmured.

'More like a servant, you mean? Well, that's what I was, back in Monsieur Pierre's time. Our situation was set, cast in stone, if you will, like the graves in Montparnasse. It was not necessary that our marriage disturb it. As Madame's condition developed, it was better that we marry, and practical. She needs to be cared for, and it is easier this way. Sometimes she is much worse than this, capable of going out into the street in her nightclothes. To look for Charles.'

'Does he still exist? Do *they* exist?'

'For her, certainly, but no, not now.'

Madame called me back to the table. I sat down with a mixture of wariness and ennui. The latter was always with me. I didn't want anything else to drink but Albert brought small plates of cold fish and salad. Like all good carers he'd read my mind.

'Eat, monsieur, you are our guest.'

I did and felt better.

'I'll have to go soon,' I said.

Madame Amelier seemed to look right through me now, as if she was caught in the lights of a distant past. Albert retreated to his bar and began to polish it again. I could see his pale face reflected back at him as he hummed a tune to himself. I think he was satisfied with his morning's work. Madame reached out and touched my face.

'Please, monsieur, could you turn towards the light? Yes, you *are* so much like them. I wonder what power brought you here today?'

Her hand was hesitant, and then it traced the contours of my face more confidently, like a blind person. It fell away and she was silent. I did not realise Albert had approached us again until he spoke.

'Madame is tired, monsieur,' he murmured.

I wondered if he ever called her by her first name. I wondered what it was as I got up to leave the strange bar.

'Thank you, monsieur,' Albert said. 'You coming here this day was providence itself.'

I shrugged a denial as he shook my hand. We stood in the doorway for a moment and Albert gestured to the cemetery.

'Walk there,' he said. 'Wasn't that what you originally planned?' and then, as he shut the door after me, 'keep to the left as you go in.'

I heard the key reluctantly turn in the rusty lock as I stood on the step for a moment. The heat assaulted me, the sun momentarily blinding as my eyes adjusted to the light. I noticed the name over the café door – *Albert Jannick*.

I entered the cemetery, taking a plan of the graves from the man at the booth. Only the French could overdo death so stylishly, but it was not to my taste as each grave tried to outdo the next in overblown grandeur. It seemed people who had made their mark wanted to repeat it here, forever.

I came across Sartre quite easily, a small sandstone affair close to the entrance, and De Beauvoir was alongside him. As

Madame said, she was now permanently next door. The small stones stood out in their simplicity. I walked further down, keeping to the left, as the old man had told me to do. There was another unduly modest grave close by. I read the inscription.

Pierre Amelier, died aged thirty-four, and his son, Charles, died aged twenty-one.

Nothing else. No utterances of loss or remembrance. No mention of Madame, and most noticeably, no dates. I sat on an adjacent bench. There were a few people around but the silence was crushing, as if the multiple ranks of the dead insisted on it. I felt my own loneliness, which I usually tried to pass it off as solitude. I liked the quiet though, for I knew only too well that it could be even lonelier amongst people.

I felt Madame must have wandered for some time, struck off course by the first untimely tragedy, and hopelessly foundered by the second. The bench was in the shade, and I sat on it for some time. I thought of my own losses and resignations, wondering if my mind would turn in on me one day, trapping me inside it with sad memories.

On my way back I looked in on the Bar De la Croix. It was shut up, with no signs of life inside. This time I noticed the dust on the window frames and the glass smeared with grime. It would be easy to think I hadn't been here at all, that I had fallen asleep on my cemetery bench, and that my remarkable hosts had lived only in my mind. But no, peering more closely, I saw that Albert had left the empty Ricard bottle on the table, perhaps forgetfulness, perhaps as a small marker of a sad anniversary. I made a mental note to be out this way next year, making a date with Madame Amelier. I had no doubt she would be waiting for me.

THE BEACHED WHALES

What Mark remembered most was the sudden breaking of water, the sluggish, calm surface churned, and the small boat tossed and heaved without warning. The instant island that was suddenly alongside him, a slab of charcoal shot through with a lighter grey. Encrustations of parasites bristling the great body like armour.

A family swims around him. Rear flukes spoon the water with graceful caress, and a monstrous yet subtle power flicks spray into his wondering eyes. A huge orb comes parallel to him, confirming his helplessness with its languid look. He cannot tell male from female but the children are much smaller. They dart more than glide, not having reached the weight when movement is an economy of action. Bumping against the boat they undulate away from him, then return again. They are playing with him. Mark locks the oars and lets the boat bob, sensing that he is quite safe. It is the first time in his life he feels like this.

Enveloped by their presence Mark imagines his soul turned outside of him, given shape, at first amorphous, then distilled with potency, and purpose, the ocean its amniotic fluid. Floating there forever untroubled. Safe.

Ahead, the incurious parents surge on, like vast ploughs making furrows in the dull sea, spouted plumes of water marking their progress. After a last bump of the boat the kids join them. Mark tracks the group as long as he can, his eyes greedy for every scrap of knowledge, until they bleed into the distance and the sea returns to its table of calm slate.

Slate grey. That was the colour of the old terraced house, a grey house in a grey row, one of the many that ribboned the lower slopes of the hillside. Mark does not want his thoughts to return there, to shrink back down to the meagre reality of his life. He rows back to the landing stage, setting his face against the low sun that has just shown itself for the first time. His is a pinched face, scrunched up around his eyes that are so far back in his head they are like dark slits. A pale face, dotted with spots. A face determined to speed through youth as fast as it can, until it becomes old and worn. A thin wisp of hair tries to establish itself on his upper lip and on three right hand fingers the word *MAM* is spelt out, one letter for each finger. *Mam* expands and contracts as he rows, as if signalling to him. Mark is a good rower, now that his once work-shy hands have toughened up.

McGinley is waiting for him. Mark sees the diminutive figure on the planked walkway, loud noises coming from it. As he rows into range noises become threats. Mark expects this, knowing that McGinley will say he has stolen the boat, not borrowed it.

Mark dedicated himself to thieving from the age of twelve. Stealing from cars, houses and schools. Especially schools. His own school was a favourite, the hated place he had never wanted to attend. His mother was never bothered if he went or not. When he started to bring stuff home to sell he always gave her half, which kept her sweet. She liked money as much as he did, and Mark knew she was proud of him, really. You're old before your time, she said once, when he brought her a video to replace the one the shop had taken back. She told him his father had been just as bent, which pleased Mark. He had that man's name but has never seen him. Neither had his mother, not since he'd been born.

Mark lived in the first terrace on Beech Road. It should have been number one but had always been number three. Someone's joke, he liked to think. All the streets around him were named after trees but there was no sign of any of them. Further down from the terraces sprawled the estate where most of his mates lived. Mark liked the view. You could see over the estate and the far hills down to the grey blob of the sea. It was easy to see any pigs coming up and easy to get away out the back. Many times he'd run up the hillside with its high ferns and handy hiding places. He knew every inch of it.

Mark was fourteen when his mother took up with Daniels. The weasel had started to sniff around her down the club and his mother was no judge of men, she never had been. Mark came back from a job down the valley to find Daniels lying on the sofa. Sleeping a load off like he owned the place.

'Jesus Christ,' Mark shouted at his mother, 'you're not bothering with him, are you?'

Mark stood glaring down at Daniels in the middle of the room, holding a black plastic bin bag with two videos and a garden strimmer in it. Daniels did not even wake up.

'Don't be so bloody cheeky,' his mother said, looking at

63

Daniels anxiously. He'll be stopping here as a matter of fact, from tonight.'

'Aw, fuck off, mam.'

Mark received a stinging slap to his cheek, his first for years.

'I told you not to be so cheeky. Wayne is okay when you get to know him. He can be a good laugh.'

'Yeah, he looks like it,' Mark muttered.

He thought of strimming the man's head but settled for throwing down his load and charging out. Daniels slept on.

Mark ran down to his friend Deano's place. Past the boarded up houses too far gone to repair and rent out again, the corpses of cars with their guts ripped out and a windswept accumulation of litter and dog crap. None of which bothered him.

Deano had been on the glue again. His nose was running like a little kid, and his eyes looked like they were somewhere else. Mark never bothered with the stuff. Robbing gave him more money than the others, and a trace of self-respect.

'Orright,' Deano said, looking past Mark. 'Wassup? No-one after you, is there?'

'Nah. Mam's got that prick Daniels up there. You know, that weedy sod. The one always getting pissed up the club.'

Deano's eyes tried to focus.

'Bloody 'ell,' he rasped, 'desperate, like, is she?'

Mark slumped onto the sofa, feeling its busted springs dig into him like probing metal fingers. He was calming down, as he let his strong core of bitterness take over. It made him hate but kept him calm.

'Where's everyone?' Mark asked.

'Down town.'

'Why don't you leave that poxy glue alone? You can hardly talk.'

'So what? It makes me feel good.'

'You'll end up like that Pritchard boy.'

'He was stupid.'

'Get us a cuppa then, if there's no booze.'

Mark cupped the mug of tea in his hands, letting its warmth seep through him.

'You bin out robbing?' Deano asked.

'Might have.'

Mark no longer took Deano along. He was a liability when he was on the glue.

'Someone was around here on about school again,' Deano said. 'Mam's gotta go to court.'

Mark shrugged.

'You'll be sixteen soon. They can't do fuck all then.'

Daniels was the latest of a long line of men and he went the way of all the others after a spectacular bust-up with Mark's mother. The house was like a war zone for a weekend, interrupted by several visits from the police. Mark's mother blamed him for Daniels leaving. The onus was always on Mark to get on with her new boyfriend. When he was younger they had been new *daddies*, but he was too old for that now, and too big. Mam had taken up with some violent tossers in her time. If he was lucky they ignored him when he was little. Sometimes he was not lucky.

When things like this happened Mark had to get away.

He'd walk up the hillside with his airgun. If it weren't pissing down he'd lie on his back in his combat jacket and pot a few birds. They came close after a while, when they thought he was part of the ground. He liked to see them fall out of the air, then somehow felt guilty that they did.

His mother Julie was still good looking and Mark wished she wasn't. The old bat next door had a face that looked as if it had run itself into a wall, and no one bothered her. Everyone wanted a crack at his mother. She was famous for it.

Daniels left something behind when he left, something inside his mother. Julie was not too bothered. It meant more money off the social.

Mark did not know anything about babies but he thought a sprog in the house might calm his mother down, or at least keep wankers like Daniels away. They never saw him again. Daniels continued the tradition of instantly disappearing first set by Mark's own father.

Julie had a boy and she called him Shane. He was a heller at first, bawling through every night, but Mark got used to it. When he turned sixteen and did not have to get up for the odd school appearance, things became better. Mark had been prone to implosions of anger. When they came on he raged inside, until his guts felt scoured, and his face turned as white as clenched knuckles. He imagined himself doing terrible things, anything to rid the daggers of pain behind his eyes. When he left school this side of him calmed down. A little.

Mark continued to expand his illicit career. Knowing that

the police were too stretched to bother much about him. They concentrated on druggies like Deano, people who were easy to catch. Mark Richards was not easy to catch. He was careful, and not too greedy. Steady robbing, and safe targets, that was his motto. Someone burnt down the school the summer he left, and that was the good news that set the seal on the next few years.

By the time he reached eighteen Mark had managed to save money from his deals. He had eight hundred and fifty quid in a tin box under the floorboards of his bedroom. His mother knew nothing about this; otherwise she'd be dipping into it. Mark had more money than anyone he knew, and each time he added to it he imagined a future. Something his mates never thought of, yes he imagined a future that spoke of escape.

Shane grew quickly. A big, blond, chubby, active baby who did not look anything like Daniels, which made Mark wonder somewhat. When Julie went to bingo Mark did not mind looking after his baby brother. Shane was good for getting girls. They all wanted to see the new baby and Mark did all right with these, but he was always careful. Unlike Deano, who already had a kid and a hiding from the girl's father to go with it. The estate was even more a prison for that boy now.

Mark's good times proved to be short. Months after his eighteenth birthday they shattered for good. Julie had gone out to get her hair done, having reached the age when it changed colour every month. He was left to look after Shane, now two years old. It was a warm day and they were in the garden, if the mess out back could be called that. Mark sat on the back step, smoking, and watching Shane root around in a pile of sand the council had left there. He sprayed sand up into the air with a tablespoon, gurgling with pleasure in his ready-made sand pit. Shane's hair was as light as Mark's was dark, a thatch of straw curls atop his head, kept that way by his mother. Mark thought it made his brother look like a girl.

The phone Mark had paid to be installed rang, and he went to answer it. It was the guy from Cardiff, the one who took most of his stuff. Forty quid for a video kept things moving along nicely. The man gave him lists of things to rob. Dealing with you, kid, the man said, is like going to a supermarket. When he put the phone down Mark got himself a beer from the fridge and Shane was forgotten for a few minutes. When he went back out into the garden his brother was not there.

Mark shouted for Shane, knowing that he was hiding somewhere waiting to be found, then sat back down on the step and opened the can. He sucked up the froth before it spilled out and screwed up his eyes against the sun as he tried to get some colour into his pale face. Maybe he could burn a few spots off. Slurping and shouting alternatively, Mark was annoyed that he would have to look for Shane.

He finished the can and went next door. No, the woman there hadn't seen Shane. Mark checked back and front, and the open waste ground that stretched away from his street. Shane could not have toddled out of sight, not that far in a few minutes. He must have crept back into the house. Mark searched the house, anger in his call now, but also anxiousness creeping into his mind. His shouts alerted the neighbours. Soon everybody was out looking, shouting. Mark began a litany to their questions. *I only left him for a minute.* Come on, Shane, he told himself, stop messing around, for fucksake. Anxiousness turned to alarm.

Mark checked through their tiny house again, looking in places impossibly small. Someone mentioned the police and he felt his guts churn. This was stupid. Crazy. *A minute is all it takes,* he heard a voice say. *There's some evil bastards around,* another added. Mark's brain began to bounce around in his head as his mother was getting off the bus. Alarm turning to panic.

Shane was not found and the rest of that week was a blur for Mark. It was a haze of questions, accusation, tears and anger. All the world on his back. Mark went over it countless times, with the police, then a shrink that was brought in. How long had he left Shane, one minute, two, ten, half a day? Even his mother was not sure about him. That he might have done something terrible. How could she think that? No one had seen anything strange. No one weird around. No cars, no nothing. And the busy police, the countrywide searches and media appeals yielded the same nothing. Shane seemed to have vanished into the spring air.

They talked to Deano, who told them how Mark had hated Daniels. So maybe he hated that man's son too. Two plus two equals fucking four. Daniels himself was banged up, so he was out of the frame. There were two weeks of questioning, a slow, burning hell that made Mark draw further into himself than ever, and he did not want to come out again. He did not see the point. His innocence was pleaded until the words were threadbare, stripped of any real meaning until he hardly believed them himself. If that bastard phone had not rung, if, if, if. Mark tried to grab at the word like it was a saviour, but always it slipped away from him.

Then it was over. That Shane was never found was Mark's deliverance and his torture. No one bothered with him afterwards. His mother started drinking big time and he went back to thieving. But not like before. He was reckless now, doing places he would never had considered before. He was willing himself to get caught and amazed at how long it took.

A year after Shane's disappearance Mark's case came to court. The estate loved it as much as the papers, for Shane loomed large again. Julie did not attend the court. A wall of suspicion had been thrown up between them when Shane vanished, and it never came down. Mark was glad to be put away.

Mark did not tell McGinley about the whales. He did not want to share the experience with anyone. He endured ten minutes of bellowing from the Scot, McGinley using the phrase *last chance* like a demented preacher. Mark was not interested. Losing Shane had taken away any notions of *chances*.

McGinley's place was meant to be a reward for Mark. For keeping his head down and behaving himself at the young offenders' place. They called this a *positive response* and were satisfied. He knew they wanted to be told they were right, that their system was right, so that they could feel good about their own shitty lives.

Mark shut down after McGinley's first sentence. It was too much of an effort to understand the man when he was angry. His accent was a whine that came from the middle of the throat. Mark angled his head away from McGinley's to avoid his tiny projectiles of spittle, and let his words be taken by the wind that was getting up.

Mark had first glimpsed the whales off the island a week ago. At first he was not sure if they were just chance happenings of shadow and light, but McGinley confirmed the sighting. He came dancing down the walkway like a kid and told Mark that it was the time for the whales that had been coming here for generations. *Here* being somewhere in The Shetlands, an Outward Bound Centre, used by the rich and now home to the occasional scally like Mark Richards. It was the big new idea from the authorities that had amazed Mark, and he liked it, because it wound so many people up. He had read about himself in the papers, about how much people like him were costing the taxpayer.

McGinley had gotten under Mark's skin instantly, to the point where he had thought of driving the man's Range Rover into the sea. Now he could not be bothered, he had been close enough to whales to feel their breath. They had made him feel so small, but not useless. In fact he had felt more encouraged and sure about himself.

Mark had a room to himself at the centre. From his window he could look out to sea, to the channel that flowed between the mainland and the island. The channel the whales used. His month's stay here was coming to an end.

McGinley would write a report saying he had robbed a boat and he would be banged up again. Julie did not want him back anyway.

The dream came back that night. The whales had set Mark's mind racing, and when that happened it always raced back to Shane. He saw the twisting revolutions of his face in that May sunshine, the sand-spinning spoon, his wedge of blonde hair constantly re-arranging itself. Then he heard the hot words of his blind panic.

This time the dream was different, and much worse. He was taking Shane away from the house, quietly, checking that no stray eyes were around. They walked over the wasteland at the back of the terraces, Mark crouching down behind the remnants of a hedgerow. Shane's hand moist in his, moist and trusting, the kid gibbering away excitedly at this unexpected adventure. Lifting him over a fence and into the partially landscaped pit workings. To that gash in the ground he had found years ago with Deano. It was an air outlet for one of the old pit shafts. They used to drop stones down it, but they never heard them land. Only a windy silence escaped from its blackness. Getting stones and telling Shane what a good game this was. Kicking at the hole with his feet, widening it. Not knowing what he was going to do until it was done. Shane falling like a stone, but nowhere near as silent.

Mark came out of the dream with a denial on his lips, sweat covered but as cold as ice. He got up and felt the pain behind his eyes, and the moisture that was gathering in them. This was how it had always been. If he had ever been able to grasp one moment of joy something quickly crushed it out, killed it.

Mark sat on the chair by his window. The afterglow of the moon passing behind clouds was the only light in the room. He could just see its edge, a thin yellow lip just moving out of sight. He sat there and shivered for the rest of the night.

Mark went out very quietly at first light, descending the wooden fire escape at the rear of the sleeping quarters, He felt the light breath of a breeze that smelt of the sea and he licked at his top lip instinctively. It was a still dawn, with a strange absence of seabirds. Usually they pierced each new day with raucous insistency, but not this day. Mark screwed up his face against the brightening sky and recognised this quiet. It was too heavy, as if something was at its edge. Waiting to break in and destroy. It was the same quiet he had known in the garden, when he realised that Shane was not there.

A sliver of beach stretched away from the buildings, a thin band of sand that banked into deep water. Mark walked towards it, looking down and not more than a few feet ahead. He had learned this on the estate, keep your head down, and don't stare at anybody. It was hard to get out of the habit.

Mark did not see the beached whales until he was almost on them. Three humped bodies had been washed up on the tide. Mark was startled, expecting them to rise up at him, but they were quite still. He prodded the smallest with his foot, trying to loosen the covering over the eye. He wanted it to spring back into life and thought it might when he dared touch it. They must have come ashore at daybreak, he thought. He looked out to the channel and wondered if these were the same whales he'd rowed with, the same family. He felt tightness in his chest and his breathing was shallow. It was hard to equate these inert lumps with what he had seen swimming yesterday.

There was a noise behind him. McGinley was running towards him, shouting again.

'My God,' McGinley said, 'three of them. I can't believe it. They do this, you know. One gets sick, disorientated, maybe, and heads for the shore. The rest follow. No-one knows why.'

Mark did not answer.

'Perhaps the family bound is too strong to break,' McGinley said, quieter this time. The Scot took out a tape measure and began to size up the bodies. 'This one must be ten tons at last.'

Mark stepped towards McGinley and took him by the shoulder, sinking his fingers into his flesh. McGinley staggered and lost his footing but Mark held him up.

'I don't know what happened,' Mark yelled. 'Why can't people understand that? I don't know what happened.'

The thick Welshness of his voice spoke of closed-in valleys and minds, and sounded alien in this open, watery place. McGinley looked up at him, incomprehension and fear in his eyes.

'Don't know what happened,' Mark repeated, this time his voice dying to a whisper. He let McGinley fall to the wet sand and turned back towards the whales.

PUSHOVER

The crowd surged past Elkins' window. For him it was a beast with snarling, ragged edges, the souls of a thousand people condensed into one mind, one will powered by a collective strength. A part of the edge broke away. It became two young men who fell into his garden, bouncing over the top of his privet hedge as if it wasn't there. They laughed and shook their cans of lager, making them miniature fire extinguishers to squirt over each other.

Elkins ducked behind his curtains as eyes probed his window. As one, the youths unzipped their tight jeans and sprayed his front door like animals marking out a territory. Elkins flattened himself against a wall and squinted through the gap in the curtain.

He had not seen the crowd detach into individuals before. No one had ever been this close. *That they might try to enter.* The thought struck home and an old, cold sweat came back, terrible and familiar, touching his soul with ice and memories. The boys, and to him they were boys, seemed robotic in their actions and their dress. Tight blue jeans stretched over their legs like an extra skin, and hair cropped close to their skulls, so close it looked like their heads had been shaved into helmets. Perhaps this was the fashion now.

The old desire to wish himself invisible came over Elkins.

He willed the wall to suck him into it, to make him unreachable. What a relief that would be. *That they might try to enter.* The thought had immobilised him, and he hated the weakness that had haunted him all his life.

The boys were called by others and went lurching out through the front gate to join the throng, turning back for a moment to throw their cans against his front door. They became the one will again and the noise peaked now, a street exercising of lungs without any apparent connection to thought. Elkins knew this, too. By God he did.

Wales, *Walia*, had been all but unknown to him in 1946. It had just the briefest of references in his Krakow schoolbooks. The south was a dirty and industrialised part of Britain, the books said, and the country was linguistically bizarre. It was not England. Elkins thought that sounded a lot like Poland, but Wales had been a very alien place to him back then. Yes, alien, but safe. So wonderfully, fantastically safe.

Cardiff was a city adjusting to the anti-climax of victory and the knowledge that difficult lives would roll back into place once more. Normality would ensue, and with it boredom and responsibility.

The local Jewish community placed him with Gold, a jeweller with the right name for his work. Some years later Elkins achieved his own modest shop. In the docks that still bustled then he created an oasis of calm, symbolised by the stuffed and glazed tortoise he placed in his window. It was raised on a plinth that rotated slowly and Elkins built a clock into the base of the plinth. Clocks were his passion, and he became a watchmaker *par excellence.* The tortoise's regular and orderly marking of time became the trademark of his new life.

The match was in progress. Elkins heard the swell of massed voices coming from the ground, baiting, cajoling, and threatening. They shouted for a game, but he heard Berlin, Munich, and saw the gates of Oswiecim closing on him as he trudged through them with the others from the train. Glad to be out of the stink and squalor of that shuttered freight box, but glad for only the most fleeting of moments. That had been a fine day, cotton wool clouds floating slowly across a cobalt blue sky, and Mahler's Fifth playing through crackling speakers as they were urged along. Elkins delayed for a few seconds and tried to look about him, but was quickly encouraged to move on by a Dobermann that was almost rabid. He had a round bite-sized scar on his calf to prove it.

Elkins read the gate's welcoming words, and drew a scrap of false comfort from them, until someone large and shaven-headed bellowed orders at him in German. Shaven-headed like the youngsters in his garden. He was pushed into a shuffling line, just avoiding the snapping jaws of another angry guard dog. He received his filthy pyjama-like striped work suit, dead man's pyjamas he found out later, and caught the pervading smell all around him, an acrid infestation of the nostrils, the stench of sweat and fear, of the opening of bladders and bowels. Something was burning too.

An officer looked Elkins up and down. You are young, he was told, and that is good. Good for you, *der Jude.* Some whimpered as the old and young were divided up and led away. Elkins looked at the faces around him. They looked like the sheep he used to see as a boy, on their way to the slaughterhouse that was in his neighbourhood. Animals herded along the street, unaware and bewildered creatures, and all wide-eyed with fear.

Elkins closed his eyes as he tried to block these memories out. He was soaked through with sweat, but became calmer and breathed more easily. He came away from the window and went into his tiny kitchen to put the kettle on. Wasn't that what the British did, in times of stress, make a cup of tea? He had never got the habit, he preferred coffee, sharp and strong, and made the old Krakow way. Elkins poured his cup of coffee from his old pewter coffee pot and took it into his equally small front room and let its warmth soothe his shaking cupped hands.

Elkins still had that tortoise clock. The tortoise was still now but it would always be with him, a last minute salvage from his closing business. He gave the chrome plinth a quick polish and caught a clouded image of himself reflected back. It was a long, thin face in which red-rimmed eyes were framed by wire glasses and his skin was chalky from a life indoors. He had a prisoner's pallor. Add a skullcap, intensify the eyes and elongate the stubble of his chin beard and you had every caricature that had lived down the ages. Those demons from medieval times, the sub-human species that featured in Nazi films.

Elkins groaned as he sat down. His bones hurt increasingly, and the limp in his left leg became more prominent as he aged. He compared himself with the rippling, raw-boned power he'd just seen in his garden. Hopeless. It had always been hopeless. He knew that age did not come alone.

Kev's voice was hoarse. City had lost again. Wankers, that's what they were, overpaid wankers. There were only a couple of games left now and they looked like going down. It had churned his guts as the first goal had gone in, but the thought of the next home match cheered him up somewhat. It was against their oldest and nearest rivals, the derby everyone looked forward to, and it had always been a fertile breeding ground for the violence he liked to provide.

The effects of the morning's beer had been shouted off and Kev wanted more. He wanted that ice cold liquid to cool the heat he always felt inside, at least cool it for a while, until it fought back and rose effortlessly to the surface again, looking for an out.

Waiting for Dean to catch up with him, Kev leant against the wall of the pub and spat into the road. He sent out a series of wet projectiles, each one travelling a little further. His taut frame wore the blue shirt of his team, and the regulation high, laced-up boots. He liked to think he had weapons on both feet. Fair hair was cropped so close to his head it looked like shadow and each arm was tattooed. Dean had them all over his body but Kev didn't fancy that. Dean was a big stupid bastard, but good in a rumble.

Kev ached for a bit of violence, but it was getting harder, with the pigs kitted up with their fucking cameras and the like. He saw himself as old school, hanging on to old head-crunching ways. Dean appeared, looking like a muscle-bound tattoo as he approached. A large part of his body art was a large bluebird that curved from his shoulder to the side of his neck, like a birthmark from hell flying towards his face.

'You getting 'em in or what?' Kev said. 'I'm fuckin' skint.'

They crashed into the pub, to be saluted by their mates. The pub was a fortress. Their fortress. It was built like a war bunker, low, squat and grey concrete-ugly outside, and inside. Its decor was worn, sepia photographs of old footie on its walls, and a floor covering so sticky with spilt beer it did not want to release the feet of drinkers. The police insisted that all drink here was served in plastic glasses. Kev resented that. Who the fuck did they think they were?

'Did you see that old geezer in that poxy flat?' Kev muttered, as he quickly sank half of Dean's proffered pint.

'What flat?'

'Down the road. Where we had that slash. He thought I couldn't see his mug behind that curtain. Sad old git, he was. I hate 'em. Should be put down before they get like that. No point in 'em being alive, if you call that being alive.'

'Shuffling old bastards,' Dean added.

Dean liked to add phrases of support to Kev's sentences. Often he didn't understand what his friend was saying, but he liked to share in the glory of Kev's words because Kev was a top bloke, someone to look up to.

Kev's pint lasted another two swallows and he split the plastic glass down its side when he banged it down onto the bar. Twenty of Kev's disciples laughed and began to chant.

'Where's that geezer with that mobile phone thing,' Kev shouted over the din. 'We'll have to nick a few of them, Deano, they gonna be all the rage in a few years.'

Another minion, better dressed than the others, handed

him the large phone. Kev liked it. It was black and looked very military, with it in his hand he felt cool, and he made sure all the boys knew it. The phone would be handy in a fight too, for it was like a small house brick, just right for pushing through someone's teeth.

After a splutter of static Kev got through to his opposite number at the rival club. They set up the meet for the morning of the last match, like businessmen closing a deal. When he handed the phone back Kev felt a rush of excitement, his fists opening and closing in anticipation of the action to come. This time they were meeting up miles from the London ground and he hoped that would fool the police, who would be out in force after last year. They would go up in small groups this time, and then come together quickly.

Kev screwed up his small eyes and smiled, he was pushing that geezer's head into that wall again, feeling his flesh give way to the rough stone, then letting him slip to the ground in a bloody heap whilst he ran at the next man, boots and fists flailing. He'd lost the tip of his right ear that day but he loved the scar it had left. It was like the best fucking earring of all time.

He could taste old and future violence, the shaking charge of it when things went well, or even if they didn't. It was all the same for him, as long as the pigs weren't involved. If he went down for a third time it would be for a long stretch. They didn't like triple artists. Action made him feel alive. Like he was somebody. Flying high with his violent moves. It made life worthwhile for the briefest of moments.

'C'mon,' Kev said to Dean, 'let's go up to town. We can get a bit of practice in for London. You can pay for the taxi.'

The club was heaving, like it was one rutting beast. Crowded bodies were in close, sticky proximity, most of the girls in fuck-me dresses two sizes too small, and the men in short-sleeved shirts dripping with sweat and testosterone. It was getting on for midnight and Kev could see that most in here were pissed, and a fair few wasted on crack or tabs, or whatever they could get their hands on. He was stone cold sober and that was how he liked it, for it gave him an edge over every bozo in this place.

Kev smirked as he watched Dean barge his way to the bar, a thin curl of his even thinner lips. All Kev's features were stripped down and ferret-like, built for evil and sniffed-out opportunities. A few took exception to Dean's bullocking progress but thought better of it when they checked out his bulk. Dean returned with two spilling pints of lager, complete with froth moustache.

'How much?' Kev shouted over the din. 'For two fuckin' pints? Good job you were paying, Deano. Right, les have a look round. See them two gits over there, that's right, the ones in the corner dressed like shit. They couldn't pull if they were here all week, and I don' like the way that tall one is looking at me.'

'He ain't looking over here, Kev.'

'Well I think he is – so he is, right?'

'Sure, Kev – the fuckin' bastard.'

'Well, keep your eye on 'em. When they go we go. Right, hold my pint, I'm gonna have a bop.'

Kev's moved into a group of dancing girls and began to gyrate amongst them, oblivious to their looks of disgust.

'Hey, whatdya thinks girls, John Travolta or what?'

'John revolting more like,' one of them shouted back.

This animated Kev even more, Dean watching him in admiration with a pint in each hand. Kev whirled around, making sure he bumped into the gobby girl, his eyes wild but all-seeing, and they saw his two targets preparing to leave the club. He stopped moving, like a circuit suddenly shut down, went back to Dean, downed his pint in ten seconds and told Dean to follow him. Not that Dean needed telling. Following Kev was a big part of his life, the most important part.

The club emptied into a rear lane, full of fast food shit, guys pissing up against the wall, and one girl sitting head down in the gutter with vomit forming a small lake in the lap of her dress.

Kev followed the two men as they made their way down the alley, waiting until they were out of range of the club's CCTV.

'Here, mate,' Kev shouted, 'got a light?'

As the man turned Kev hit him hard in the face. The man was a good head taller than he was, which made it all the sweeter. He felt teeth shatter against hard bone, and the man fell back. His friend stepped in to intervene and was tackled by Dean, who put two large hands on his shoulders and lifted him off his feet. The man kicked out and caught Dean on a knee, which was unfortunate for him. He was thrown against the uneven wall, sinking down with a heavy thud. His night's entertainment was over but Dean added a few kicks as an afterthought.

Kev was not doing so well. His target was strong and fit, and had got over the surprise to punch back and pin Kev against the other well. He felt stone graze against the back of the head as the man hit him hard in the gut, which encouraged the lager to come back up.

'You little oink,' the guy shouted.

Yeah, Kev liked that, a ponce accent that reddened further the mist forming before his eyes.

'Deano,' he shouted, 'for fucksake.'

Dean was there, effortlessly dragging the man off, breaking his hold on Kev so that his leader could go to work with his boots. Each kick to the body, then face, was like a line of coke to Kev. Happiness surged through him, he was Superman unleashed. Despite the gloom of the back alley he could see the blood pouring out of the man, making his face a dark sodden mass, which Kev trained his right boot on.

'Kev! Kev! You're gonna kill him.'

People were running towards them. A few bouncers from the club who had been attracted by the noise.

'Okay, okay,' Kev shouted back. 'We're gone. Them fat fuckers will never catch us anyway.'

And they didn't. They had disappeared into another alley and out into the next road whilst the clubmen stopped to pick up the pieces.

'I enjoyed that,' Kev said. 'Am I hard or what?'

Kev howled into the night sky and didn't hear Dean's answer. But he wondered what an oink was.

Elkins was glad that the football season was almost over because he could not avoid walking past that pub they used. It was the only way he could get home from the shops, unless he took a taxi, and that would never do. There was a young man outside the pub doors now as he approached, a figure vaguely familiar though he only dared a short glance up. He avoided looking directly at him, in a way he had learned so well it was etched into his character. Unseeing eyes had been his one defence, the ability to never look at any of them unless it was absolutely vital. When it had been, he'd willed his eyes to melt into nothingness, and say that their owner was not worth bothering about. To tell them he was just an insignificant stain on the glorious Nazi empire and could be blotted out later. Any time. It was humility taken to its extreme, allied to his youth. He was able to work on whilst others dropped, doing what was necessary to survive. It had kept him alive in that hellish place which the world called by its German name now.

Elkins had been to the post office to send letters. Letters kept him going, and made the course of his life a little easier. He wrote to three people, Krygiel, in New York, Kowalski in Tel Aviv and Rita Bloom, who had arrived at the camp in those final few weeks and had been overlooked in the last rush of murder. Rita was the only one of them who had managed to integrate. She lived in Manchester, where she had raised a large family. He had a collection of photographs she had sent him over the years. Black and white, then colour as they charted her history. Rita's life had been full and he was glad for her, though not without a touch of envy. Rita had managed to move on better than most of them. Next year was the start of a new millennium and it looked like they would all reach it. They were three minor miracles in a savage world.

Elkins played chess with Krygiel. The professor had beaten him just twice in forty years. When Elkins played chess he immersed himself in its strategies and saw the routes to victory with a confidence he could not countenance in real life. He was close to checkmate now, and had been thinking of the last killer move for three days. No hurry. Let Krygiel stew a little. You should have taken it up seriously, Krygiel had urged. People make money at it now. But Elkins never did. There had never been enough time.

It was time for the crew's London trip. Kev was in the back seat of the first car, Dean up front with Carl the driver. Carl was the smallest in the crew but very capable. He'd been done for stabbing someone once, which gave him extra street cred, and even Kev was a bit wary of Carl.

It was very early Saturday morning, a grey, drizzly spring day.

'Fuck me' Kev muttered, 'can you believe people get up at this time every day – stupid sods.'

'Yeah, stupid sods,' Dean echoed.

They were in south London by ten, assembling at the rear of a closed-down and deserted warehouse complex, young men stretching stiff limbs after the long drive. Kev surveyed his troops and was satisfied. Starting out at six in the morning and staying off the motorway had fooled the pigs, even if the B roads took a lot longer. Yeah, they were all early birds all right, and each one was going to get his worm.

Kev saw thirty eager, battle-hardened soldiers, most wiry and fit and not very tall. Kev had met a guy once down the Fortress who had told him that most men in the SAS were not that tall either. He liked that; in his fervent head it meant there was some sort of connection there. Yes, they too were warriors, warriors on a mission.

Kev's team gathered around him.

'Smell that air, boys,' he shouted, 'what does it smell of?'

'Violence!' was the united response.

'Who are we? Who are we?'

The crew took up the chant; it was their primitive call to action. Plenty of cans had been drunk on the trip up; adrenalin was coursing through primed bodies just as the rival team came around the corner. It was a stand-off for a long minute, each group a mirror image of the other, a tangled collection of shaven heads, denim, Burberry and Doc Martin's. Regulation gear. Only the accents were different. Then it happened, as if a switch had been flicked in each head.

Kev ran at the guy he knew was their leader, with Dean his wingman. Kev liked to have that bulk close to him. At eighteen stones Dean was easily the biggest man here and he ploughed through the London boys easily, allowing Kev to get to his target. Kev grabbed the man by his collar and pulled him towards him. He felt a sharp kick in his side from someone else, but Dean dealt with that. He heard a dull, crunching thud and a man went down quickly.

Kev's opposite number was good and broke Kev's hold, smashing a short jab into his face. He felt an eye instantly start to close which was all the pain he needed to get him to the next level. He dragged the man down and started punching and kicking, maybe biting. He didn't know because all he saw was a red blur in front of his eyes as hatred poured out of him. Like a devil that had to be served. He loved it. He hated it. Yeah, most of all he hated it. Hated the way it controlled him, the way it told him to pay back the world for all the crap in his life. His useless slut whore junkie mother and all her useless fucking men. His poverty and the shithole he lived in. He hated it for telling him he should never have been born, for knowing that he was an evil bastard. And never letting him forget it.

Kev's opponent stopped struggling. His wild-eyed face was a bloody mess, but Kev hit it a few more times anyway. Other men were trying to get to him, but Dean batted them all away. With Dean standing over him Kev sat in the dirt and saw all the action around him, men pairing off in almost balletic routine to have their own personal wars. There were no knives or chains here, no weapons of any kind — just fists and feet, the code of all the crews. They were gentleman, after all.

'Pigs!' someone shouted above the battle din, 'vans coming down the road!'

Others took up the cry. Despite the intensity of the fight, action was cut off quickly as the two groups disengaged and tried to get away. Police vans were speeding towards them from an access road, and men scattered everywhere. Kev led the way. He was glad the police had finally got here. It gave a stamp of approval to the action. Followed by Dean and a few others, Kev was back in the car and away before the police got anywhere near. Four bloodied figures laughing their way home, Kev throwing back his head and whooping as he fed off the buzz of the brawl. None of them thought much about the football match that would later take place.

Kev's crowd adopted the Fortress as their summer watering hole. They were there the last Saturday of May when the season was over and the action had cooled.

'What we doing this summer then, Kev?' a voice asked.

'Dunno what you lot are doing but I'm going on the rob again. I've had a gut's full of being skint. That giro is only good for one night's piss-up.'

'We doing cars again, Kev?' Dean asked.

'Cars be fucked. Nah, that's yesterday, that is. They got too much security now, and every bugger's got a radio.'

'What then?'

'Houses, innit. Got to be. And shops maybe. We don' need nothing to ram raid 'em with. We can use Dean.'

Kev turned to the long table of faces that laughed on cue. He left the table and took Dean into a corner.

'Listen, you was from round here, before you come on the estate. What's the crack?'

Dean looked at him blankly.

'Jesus wept,' Kev said, 'I forget how thick you are sometimes.'

He tapped Dean's head and pretended to look inside his ear. Dean grinned.

'This part of town used to be posh years ago,' Kev said.

'Maybe there's a few of them fuckers left, sitting on their notes as well as their stinking old arses.'

'There's pensioners, like, down them flats by the ground.'

Kev thought back a few weeks.

'Aye, that old sod in the window. Nah, he looked piss-poor, he did. Gemme a pint.'

Kev went out to the pub's entrance. He liked to stand in the doorway when there was a bit of sun, and feel like he owned something. By the time he was twenty he had given up on work. Why not, it had given up on him. At twenty-three he was the oldest in the group, and his worn, pinched face was already turning its back on its youth. He looked as if he had been born with the blue smudges under his eyes.

Kev looked down the street to the flats. At least they would have videos, which were good for fifty bucks. Dean brought out the beer, sloshing some of it on the pavement.

An old man was coming down the road on the other side. Kev stared across at the man and spat into the street. The man had an overcoat on, something that had been expensive once. He gave no sign that he was aware of Kev and tried to fade into the road as he passed on quickly, limping on his left side, his eyes stuck to the floor like eggs to a pan. Old bugger's afraid of me, Kev thought, with a touch of pride. If it had been dark he might have considered a mugging. There was something about the old git. Fuck, aye. From that flat down the road. He followed him down to it with his eyes to make sure.

'We going to town, or what?' Dean asked.

'Aye, might as well. But we'll be back down here later.'

Kev drank what money Dean had. Beer was a problem. The more he drank the more he could take. It cost a lot now to get pissed. He'd only had six pints, but it was enough to make him feel meaner than usual. Mean enough to hate his poverty, and blame everyone and his brother for it.

'Come on, brain dead,' Kev said, 'let's go back down our place.'

Dean followed Kev across town.

'How much you got left?' Kev asked

Dean held out a hand with assorted coins in its palm.

'Fuckin' hell, less than a quid. That settles it. I'm going down the road tonight, down them flats.'

'What we gonna do, Kev?'

'You ain't gonna do nothing 'cept keep a look out. And sort anyone out that needs it. We'll try that old sod with the coat first. Get his video and sell it on the estate in the morning.'

'How much we get?'

Kev thought for a moment.

'Thirty quid. You can have ten.'

They hung around the pub as long as they could, then walked down the street when it had emptied of drinkers. Kev sauntered down the road, pushing back his shoulders and grinding his hands in his pockets. Dean padded along at his side, his human Rottweiler. Kev could taste the coming action and felt like someone again.

Kev's malevolent stare had disturbed Elkins. It was the catalyst to spark another cycle of recall, in what had been a year of deadly anniversaries. First Auschwitz, then Belsen.

Others would follow in a chronology he found hard to deal with. The massed candles on the railway tracks, *his* tracks, had moved him, but also stripped naked his guilt. The guilt that he had survived into another world, and that he had wanted to do so. But it was a world that had not learned. If the Holocaust could not encourage permanent change he doubted that anything ever would.

Sweat formed on his brow in small pimple-like beads. He was up late but did not want to sleep. Nightmares dwelt there. Always he saw those last days, the frenzied but methodical killing, when they no longer cared if the living were crammed into the ovens. Then came the end of it all that had never seemed possible. His eighty wasted pounds twitching in the unnatural quiet of abandonment. Hearing a bird call as it flew overhead, but not sure if this was a last trick of hell, and that *życie*, life, would still be taken from him. Waking with a sigh too tired and knowing to ever be a scream.

'Don' stop and gawk, you stupid sod,' Kev said. He nudged Dean past Elkins' flat. 'Looks like there's a back lane. We'll go round there. It'll be easier.'

They waited in the shadows until all the lights went off in the flats. Kev pushed open Elkins's back gate.

'Fuckin' rotten, that is,' he muttered. 'Just like that old fucker.'

Kev's approach was direct. A piece of house brick wrapped in Dean's jacket shattered the glass square of the back door of the flat. Kev reached inside to find the key in the lock.

'Stupid old buggers. They never learn.'

Elkins heard the glass breaking. He had almost expected it. There was something about this night. His curtains were open and streetlight cast an orange glow onto his chessboard. He had moved a knight to counteract Krygiel's last move but his old friend had not yet responded.

They did not see him at first, as they fumbled their way into the room.

'There's nuffink here,' Dean whispered, 'I can' even see no telly.'

'Shut the curtains before I put the light on. The old guy must be in bed.'

Dean was startled when he saw the tortoise. Then his groping hands probed Elkins' shadowy corner and connected with his face. He jumped back.

'Jesus Christ, there's someone there.'

Light flooded the room as Kev found the switch.

'Well well,' Kev said, 'it's granddad. What you doing sat in the dark, pop? We come to visit you, like. Don' want no trouble, do you? Nah, 'course you don't.'

Dean was confused. His fists ached to take over from his meagre thought processes but the old man looked pathetic. Kind of shrivelled, somehow.

'I reckon the old git is cracked,' Kev said.

He looked around the room and saw that Dean was right. No telly, video, no fucking nothing except books and a clapped out looking radio. Books be fucked.

'Ain't nothing here,' Dean repeated.

'I can see that, piss-brain.'

Kev brushed a row of books from the top shelf of a case.

They tumbled to the floor in a shower of dust, some so old their spines were immediately broken.

'Where d'you keep it then?' he shouted.

He pushed his face close to Elkins, showering him with beer breath spittle. Elkins saw the snarl of his imperfect teeth and found his voice.

'If it's money you want I have very little,' he said.

'You foreign or summat?'

Kev squinted at him more closely.

'I know you. You're that old git what had that poxy place down the docks. My old woman used to go there when I was a little kid. You're a Yid.'

Żyd, a word from the old country. Elkins looked through a thousand Kevs to the past.

'Not paying attention, pop.'

A stinging slap jerked Elkins's head back. Kev turned to Dean.

'We struck lucky here. He must be loaded and don' spend much either by the look of this dump.'

'He ain't got no telly,' Dean said, with wonder in his voice.

'I'll ask you one more time,' Kev said. 'I know you bastards, you'll have it stashed somewhere, away from the fuckin' taxman.'

He grabbed Elkins by his lapels and pulled him up.

'Now look, you don' want no more. See this boy here, this big bastard, he ain't right in the 'ed, see. And once he starts...'

'I tell you the truth,' Elkins said. 'I have just a few pounds in my purse.'

'A purse? Fuck me, you're a right old wuss, in' you, sunshine.'

Elkins handed the purse to Kev, who snatched it, opened it and counted out the coins.

'Eight fucking quid. You must be joking.' Kev jerked a thumb at Dean. 'Listen, this one is thick, I ain't.'

Kev's hand worked across Elkins' face a few more times. He tasted blood inside his mouth, its old, familiar salt.

'Watch him,' Kev said, 'I'm gonna have a look round.'

He rifled his way through the flat, rubbishing things noisily.

It was a long five minutes. Elkins knew that when Kev returned from his fruitless search rage would be reinforced by frustration, to create a legitimate grievance in the young man's mind. He would be diminished into a vile speck, a thing to prey on and abuse. Then Kev's actions would not only be necessary, they would be justified. Dean looked at the chessboard,

'Wassis?'

'Only a game.'

Dean picked up a queen, and twirled her carved wood in his great hands.

'Fuck off,' he said, 'them's ornaments.'

But he replaced the queen quite gently.

'Tell him where the money is,' he murmured.

Elkins saw that this bovine one was not innately dangerous. Men like him had abounded in the camp, the fodder of the small and mean, the men in control. Something in his pocket pressed against his leg, the paper knife he'd used earlier, the one Krygiel had sent him. It was a thin but strong blade with the Star of David on the handle. Kev re-entered the room.

'I can't find fuck all,' he said.

'It is how I told you,' Elkins said. 'You have picked the wrong man and the wrong place.'

'Don' you make a fool out of me, you old sod. I *know* there's money here.'

'You are too late, my young friend. Yes, I did have money, but I gave it away. To Israel.'

'Who the fuck's he?' Dean asked.

'Israel is a country, my country.'

'What's he on about, Kev?'

'Shut up, you donkey.' Kev tugged at Dean. 'You just said my name. What have I told you about that?'

'Oh yeah – sorry, Kev.'

This was getting out of control. Kev knew he was losing it. There was the familiar red blurring in his eyes, and he felt the irresistible urge to go apeshit.

'Go on, then,' Kev shouted, 'do him. Do the fucker!'

Dean was confused, and did not move.

'But he's old, though?'

'For fucksake,' Kev yelled, 'why do I bother? I'll do him myself. Come here, you old bastard.'

He jerked Elkins to his feet, lined up his face for pounding and received the paper knife between the ribs. Elkins was amazed at its ease of entry. There was a hiatus of silence, a crushing moment that made him think that there had never been noise. Kev's body seemed frozen, his face locked with shock. Then he dropped down, emitting one small gasp and a barely intelligible curse.

'What you done? 'Dean cried, 'what you done to my mate?'

He stepped towards Elkins, looked down at Kev, at the red liquid escaping from him, then back again to Elkins. It was too much for him. He crashed out of the flat, straight into the arms of the police. Elkins' neighbour had called them, when he heard the shattering of the rear door pane.

Elkins still had the knife in his hand when the police entered, his trembling fingers tracing the outline of the star. They prised it away from him. Carefully.

'Looks like the old fella flipped,' an officer said.

They cordoned off the flat and waited for CID. A sergeant arrived. He looked at Kev, at his dead staring eyes.

'Good God,' he muttered, 'it's Kevin Carl Jenkins.' He turned to Elkins. 'Want to tell us what happened, sir?'

Elkins wasn't listening. He looked out of the window. At the sky that was never really dark here for streetlights had long since blotted out the stars. Light rain had started up sometime in the night; it slicked the tarmac, making it glisten moist orange. Elkins sucked in great gulps of air like he used to do in the camp, when he thought his end had come. But this time he felt calm. So very calm. For the first time in his adult life there was an absence of fear. He was light-headed with it. Perhaps this is what calm means, he thought.

'What happened?' Elkins said. 'I fought back, that's what happened. I fought back.'

SON OF MOSES

Sighting along the barrels of the shotgun from the ridge, Moses saw the Bryn loom large. The farmhouse seemed to be skewered on the end of the black barrels, like it belonged there. He remembered a time when guns had fascinated him. The feel of them, the perfectly balanced weight in his hand, the raucous explosion inches from his ears, and the familiar smell of cordite penetrating his lungs. Even the symmetry of the red cartridges lined up on the pantry shelf pleased him. A shotgun's children, the old man called them. That was a long time ago. Now the gun felt heavy in his hands and his intentions dreadful.

Moses came to the Bryn at twenty, willing to take it on from old Jenkins as a tenant. You'll be a slave more like, his father had told him. The Bryn was fifty acres of hill cut by the east wind and pulling down all the rain from the west. The farmhouse and barn were set in a lee with a scattering of trees, and from the top ridge Moses could see the lush pastures of his lower neighbours, and the glinting terraces of the village on the valley floor.

Thomas Moses was long and raw-boned. His thin, sand-coloured hair was kept cropped short, and his face seemed to be permanently set, as if he knew his future, and was moving helplessly towards it.

Moses met Isabelle in the village. She was talking with his mother in Isaac's shop.

'This is my son Thomas,' his mother said, 'he farms up at the Bryn – *on his own*.'

Isabelle put out a hand. It was lost in his. Moses flushed a deep red. Isabelle was taller than most girls of that time, and a few years older than him. With her high shoes she could almost look him in the face. He stared at the floor and mumbled a hello.

'Isabelle is one of the Morgans from the bottom farm, Thomas. You remember the boys, don't you? She's been away working with the land army. All the way to Kent.'

This meeting stayed with Moses, and Isabelle's face came to him often as he worked, toiling in his sodden spring fields. He remembered her slate grey eyes and hair the colour of his own. He met her several more times in the village, but words came no easier to him.

Isabelle invited herself up to the farm, knowing that Moses would never ask her. He was ploughing the bottom field when he saw her pushing a bicycle along the rutted lane. He felt panic but also excitement. Somehow he managed to show her around, his pride in the farm overcoming his shyness. Megan the sheepdog fussed around his visitor. The dog liked Isabelle as much as Moses did. Moses asked her to call again, but when he sat in his kitchen, ruffling Megan's thick coat, he cursed himself for not even offering her tea.

Isabelle did call again and within weeks she was helping Moses on the Bryn, pleasing him with her knowledge of the land. By early winter they were together, the relationship reluctantly accepted by Isabelle's incredulous family. When the hay barn was full they drank cider and held hands.

'We make a good team,' Isabelle said, as she rested a shoulder against him.

They married that Christmas of '48, in the chapel at the edge of the village, Moses squirming in his ill-fitting suit and anxious to be back at the Bryn.

Moses and Isabelle tamed the farm, as much as anyone could. Moses used the pair of horses rented from Jenkins for ploughing until he achieved a third-hand tractor in 1955. When Jenkins died he was able to buy the farm from his widow, on terms that would lock him into the Bryn for life. Terms he liked.

Moses and Isabelle remained a steady couple, content in their unity and spending their lives with hard work and solitude. Others saw them as dour. In the pause between winter and spring, when farm work eased up a little, they had a brief time to walk their land, glad to be a part of it.

No child came to them in their first ten years. When Isabelle turned thirty-five this began to prey on her mind. She wanted a crop of her own, but to discuss it with Moses was useless. Of an evening, in the slim time between work and sleep he liked to sit quietly by the fire, Megan, then Tom, sprawled at his feet. Her man staring at the coals, as if they contained great mysteries and revelations. Moses used his body to talk for him, a shrug of the shoulders, a raising of eyebrows, sometimes a sigh. A vigorous attack on the fire with the poker was his sole sign of agitation.

'Wouldn't you like children, Thomas?' Isabelle asked her husband, after a time of thought.

Moses took up his poker. He knew this would require words, shifty customers that he rarely used. Isabelle laid a hand on his.

'Well?' she said.

'You've never mentioned it before.'

'No, but we're not getting any younger.'

'Children have not come. We haven't prevented them.' He prodded the fire and thought for a time. 'Perhaps we are barren, like that field under the ridge. Barren no matter what I try.'

Isabelle was glad of the *we*.

'We could see about it,' she said.

'What do you mean?'

'Go to see Doctor Ellis.'

'Don't be daft, woman. We're not cattle, to be attended to by the veterinary. What will be will be.'

Isabelle knew this would be his final word. Loneliness began to creep into her, and lay like a shadow that would not fade. Friends and a social life were not compatible with her man, she'd accepted this long since, but children, or even one child, would mean roots of their own. Someone to take her life on.

One year later, in late April, it happened. Spring was softening the outlines of the Bryn, putting weight on trees, lightening undergrowth. The sheep had lambed and it was a fitting time for her, Isabelle thought, though she wondered that it had come so late. When she was sure she told Moses.

'So there is a child on the way at last,' he said. 'It will be a lad.'

There was certainty in his voice and she hoped it would be so. The Bryn was too harsh for a girl.

That summer went well for Isabelle. Despite her state she felt lighter, her spirit released. Moses took an occasional interest, once placing a hand on her belly and pronouncing himself satisfied. The back bedroom was emptied and prepared for the baby. Isabelle painted it in bright colours.

Ellis was sent for two days into November. Moses towed the doctor's car through the quagmire of the lane and into the farmyard with the tractor. Isabelle listened to their progress for what seemed an age. The woman who served as midwife to the farming community was also in attendance.

Moses sat in front of the fire, putting together the old shotgun he'd found in pieces in the back bedroom, stopping at intervals to re-arrange the logs. He polished a gleam into the gunmetal and oiled the stock. His ears pricked to the first cry but he did not go up because he had not been called. Ellis stepped into the kitchen.

'Come up now, Moses,' the doctor said. 'You've got a healthy son, a whopper by the look of him. Nine pounds at least.'

Moses entered the bedroom, bowing his head under the low beam. The presence of two women in the room unsettled him more than the sight of his son. Isabelle held him in her arms, his wrinkled, red-faced, open-eyed son.

'Healthy, you say,' he mumbled.

'Perfect,' Ellis answered. 'He'll be as big as you one day. Bigger.'

Moses touched the baby's head, hesitantly, as if his huge hand might harm it.

'What will we call him?' he asked Isabelle.

'Henry,' she answered, 'Henry Thomas Moses.'

Moses had never seen his wife looking so radiant.

Isabelle sensed there was something wrong with Henry before she knew it for sure. He was so quiet and large, his grey eyes watching with unflinching steadiness, like a young heifer. And he was slow to react to either movement or sound. It suited Moses that he had such a quiet son, who was never angry and rarely tetchy. Henry just ate and slept. Just was. Isabelle went to see Ellis before Henry was two.

'He's so slow,' she said, 'in everything he does, or doesn't do, more like. And he shows no interest in anything. The only things he plays with is my husband's old cartridge cases.'

Ellis fingered his watch chain. He had spent ten minutes examining Henry, who let himself be handled with his usual calm, disconcerting the doctor with his unblinking stare.

'There's nothing physically wrong with him, Mrs Moses, and when you say slow, well, I don't know. He's a heck of a size for his age, but I don't think there's anything to worry about. Henry will come into his own as he gets older.'

Isabelle knew the old bachelor doctor was wrong, but Ellis was dead before it could be proved. Henry never did come into his own. When he was three Isabelle and a reluctant Moses took him down to the new general hospital, miles from their valley. What she knew was confirmed. Her father recalled another like him, far back in the family.

It was hard for her to accept, and even harder for Moses. He knew what to do with runts in litters and distressed animals, but a son who was soft in the head? He became more taciturn than ever and Henry became Isabelle's boy, her responsibility, and often, her sole companion. The night they came back from the hospital, whilst Moses was busy with the animals, she pushed back Henry's hair and talked to him. Crying softly for all three of them.

When Henry was twenty-one Isabelle organised a small celebration. Some of her nephews and nieces, for Henry was more relaxed amongst children. Isabelle's parents had died in the late sixties, perishing quickly, one very close to the other, like an over-ripe crop.

Henry sat in front of the kitchen fire and a young niece helped him open his presents. He had levelled out at six feet four, and muscle had been built up doing the one thing he was entrusted with on the farm. Chopping wood. He built up pyramids of logs in the farmyard, arcing his axe in perfect syncopation. The tool looked tiny in his great hands. Isabelle often thought there was a kind of beauty in Henry's work. He was in control, achieving something. And he never chopped himself.

Henry held a toy clumsily in his hands, a giraffe with *Happy Birthday* sewn into its neck.

'It's a cow with a big neck, Uncle Henry,' his niece said.

He stroked it and attempted a smile. His was gap-toothed, from the many tumbles he had taken around the farm when he'd followed Moses around. Now Moses only allowed him the wood. Keep him out of harm's way, he told Isabelle, and out of my way. Farms are dangerous places. Isabelle wished she had more help and lived amongst people more sympathetic to Henry's needs. She read about changing attitudes, changing treatments, and wondered if one day they would reach the Bryn.

Isabelle fell ill in '82. She could not shake off a cough and had a sense of her life ticking away before she knew for sure what was wrong with her. Which was cancer, of the lungs, despite her lifetime innocence of tobacco, and the keen fresh air of the Bryn.

Another Doctor Ellis, nephew of the first, brought her the news personally. He drove into the yard on a fine July morning in a car as shiny as the day. She tried to spare his embarrassment by saying that she had known all along. Which was true, but she had still hoped.

Isabelle kept it from Moses as long as she could, then she followed the prescribed but ineffective treatment at the hospital. She took to her bed, visited by the district nurse when it was needed. On the night she died Isabelle made Moses promise his commitment to Henry.

'He's all we've got,' she said. 'All that will live after us.'

Moses looked at the skeletal hand that he held. It had prepared for the grave already. Isabelle tried to squeeze his but her grip was nothing.

'Promise,' she gasped, 'promise he'll not go in one of those homes.'

'No. He'll always be with me. Don't worry about that.'

Her eyes urged more.

'I promise,' he muttered.

Isabelle had never been ashamed of her son but she'd always thought that Moses was. He recoiled from what he did not understand and that was their tragedy. Moses walked out blindly, leaving Isabelle to the nurse.

105

He drove the tractor to the ridge, the highest point he could take it, then held his shotgun in his hand. It was a way of calming himself. The Bryn lay beneath him, smoke curling from its chimney, white squares of washing on the line, and the slender curve of the valley leading down to the coast. Henry was chopping wood in the yard, more than they could ever use. His even cuts carried up to Moses in the crisp air. Idyllic, a town dweller might say.

Moses cursed his solitary ways, the silence that shyness had moved from habit to a way of life, a silence that had locked him into it. When Isabelle had fallen ill he'd been afraid, a desperate fear that now threatened to overwhelm him. She'd wasted away so quickly. And now she was going from him, and still his silence endured. He knew it now for the fraud it was. It was weakness, selfishness. A long concealing of himself he should have fought against. He put the shotgun behind the tractor's seat and fired up the engine again.

Moses' sister Sian sat with Isabelle in the last weeks. She stayed at the Bryn for a few days after the funeral, fussing him with kindness and seeing to Isabelle's things. Henry kept to his axe work but it was not neat now. He slammed the blade into the logs unevenly, gouging out ragged chunks. When indoors he padded around the kitchen, asking for his mother. No one could explain to him the permanence of his loss. And no one dared try.

'You can't manage here on your own,' Sian said, 'not with Henry as well.'

'I promised Isabelle that I'd always look after him.'

'Henry needs constant watching. You can't do it and run

the Bryn.' She took her brother's arm. 'You see that, don't you?'

Moses let Sian take charge. She fixed the meals that Henry ate, though he took no notice of her. The arrangements concerning Henry went smoothly, the authorities admitting the impossibility of him staying at the Bryn. Moses was not badly off now, and could make a solid contribution to the state's costs.

'There's a place down the valley,' Sian said. 'You'll be able to go and see him. Get you off the Bryn for a bit.'

Moses stared at her, thinking of his promise.

'And I was talking to my Edward,' Sian continued. 'He said we could merge the Bryn with our place. If we ploughed up some of the hedges think of the size fields we could have.'

In the weeks leading up to Henry's placement Moses agreed to everything Sian suggested. At night he sat with his son, who became more at ease with him, the father who'd been a stranger. Moses found himself talking, opening up to his mute audience. They'd sit in the kitchen with the dogs; the Bryn had two now. Henry slumped in the armchair, a slouch of unfocused power. As he talked Moses cleaned the shotgun, Henry fingered some of the cartridges and smiled.

'You used to do that when you were a baby,' Moses said. 'You're a baby still.'

The day before Henry was due to be taken Moses waited for Sian to go. She was bubbling over with talks of the future. He watched her drive off in her Land Rover then took two cans of petrol and splashed the contents around the farmhouse. Henry followed him, sniffing at the petrol. Moses made sure all animals were outside then fired the house.

107

Henry was alarmed by the whoosh and clung to his father as they went outside. The dogs ran around, wild-eyed, trying to flatten themselves into the ground. Moses locked the front door and led Henry to the barn.

He put the wooden bar in place on the inside of the double doors and sat Henry on a bale. The barn was a warm haven, with sunlight shafting through a few gaps in the roof. It smelt earthy, earthy with life. He stroked Henry's head until the farmhouse was well alight. There were small explosions as the roof went up and flames escaped the shattered windows. It must have been noticed by now, he thought. People would be rushing up from neighbouring farms. That would be the first time anyone would be in a hurry to get to the Bryn.

In a few minutes Moses tried to offer Henry all the kindness he'd been unable to show him in his life. He stroked his head with calloused hands and whispered to him as he would a horse with a broken leg. Henry laid his great head on his chest placidly as he brought the shotgun up from its hiding place. His fingers curved around the trigger and it was as if the mechanism had the weight of the entire world. The blazing farmhouse and maddened dogs were blotted out. Moses moaned and shook as he fought the trigger. Fought his whole life and its destructive silences. He thought his son might also resist as his eyes locked onto the gleaming barrel, but Henry didn't move as the gun was put to his head.

ON TOP OF THE WORLD

The skin on Rob's knuckles disintegrates as he begins to slide. He grabs at stone, his boots swinging wildly, the mooned night alive in his eyes, and his heart hammering against his chest as the estuary looms large with its curve of silver light. Fat stars tease him as he steadies himself, flat against the wall, willing his torn fingers to hang on. He thinks of falling, being dashed on the rocks, drowned in the sucking sea, in that line of shit that always carries across the bay. Then he starts to climb again.

Rob pulls up his visor as Todd approaches. He switches off the petrol strimmer as sweat trickles down the back of his neck into his T-shirt.

'You should have finished this by now,' Todd says.

Rob faces his boss and forces down a grin. Todd is short and corpulent, his eyes red-rimmed, his nose made purple with whisky, his failing hair propped up with gel, and he wears a florid tie to match his florid face. But Todd is quick moving, and quietly sly when on the prowl. Rob did not hear him coming. Five minutes earlier and Todd would have caught him smoking, his back against a wooden chalet wall, thinking of Roxanne, and anywhere but Laugharne.

'I've almost finished,' Rob says

'Those new people will be here soon.'

Rob knows Todd is not talking directly to him. He's thinking about deals, profit, or just breaking even. Milkwood Timeshare, Todd's dream, has been up and running for ten years, then jogging, now limping. It's almost lame, an avaricious eighties child now old and tatty. Todd is worried.

'If you think you can possibly finish this, get down to the site entrance and cut the grass on both sides. *Not* the flowers this time.'

'Aye aye, Mr. Todd.'

'Oi, not so cocky. There's plenty of lads around here to do your work.'

Not at what you pay me there's not, you fat git, Rob mouths silently at Todd's back. He starts up the strimmer again. Midges cloud above him as they plan their attack. His body is long, lean, muscled, hair red, wiry and cropped. He's born and bred in the town.

'Your young man's outside,' Mrs. Judd says. Mrs. Judd, landlady, runs a tacky tourist tavern, and trades on myth. She stands behind the bar, flicking a brawny arm at a solitary fly.

'He gets on my nerves,' Roxanne says, 'always coming 'round checking up on me.'

'He can get on *my* nerves anytime. Good-looking lad, Rob is. Tall. I like a tall man.'

Roxanne grimaces but still checks her hair in the mirror before Rob enters. She straightens her yellow top, smooths her jeans and turns away from the door.

'Alright, Mrs. J?' Rob says, 'gimme a pint. It's hot out there.'

'It is, Rob love. There should be more visitors on a day like this.' She nods to Dylan's framed photograph on the wall. It's black and white, and cheeky Caitlin is alongside him, almost dwarfing the elfin Thomas. 'You'd think there'd be more coming to find out about that silly sod, wouldn't you, on a nice day like this.'

Rob sidles down the bar to Roxanne.

'What you doing for dinner?'

'Staying here.'

She pouts, and examines her nails.

'No, you get out for a bit, love, get a bit of sun,' Mrs. Judd says.

Rob drains his pint quickly, spilling some down his T-shirt. It adds to the sweat marks already there.

'Les' go down the castle,' Rob says. 'They won't charge me to go in.'

It's only a few minutes walk to the recently re-opened castle. There are flowerbeds inside, displays, gravel paths, a shored up part, and a crumbling section that hangs precariously over the estuary.

'Christ, people pay a few quid to see this,' Rob mutters.

'It's our heritage.'

'Our what? Oh aye, Todd talks about that, says it's a good earner, or used to be. People are getting fed up with his crappy time shares now. He can't sell 'em. Les' sit over there.'

'We're living in a famous place.' Roxanne says. 'That's why people come here.'

'It's a hole. An' how many locals in the shop down the square? None, that's how many. Just outsiders coming to take a piece of us, making dosh out of that poet ponce – and he wasn't from here, neither.'

'Well, *he's* the reason *we're* working.'

'Aye, slave workers.'

'Christ, who got out of bed the wrong side then? All you do is moan these days.'

Rob gets up, kicks the heads off a few flowers.

'I'm bored, and Todd is on my back like a crab all day. Wanna do something tonight, Rox? Go to Swansea? I'll get the old girl's car.'

'You haven't passed your test yet.'

'So?'

They indulge in a few minutes of groping. Roxanne encouraging, then mock resisting, but Rob is eager. He is always eager. Elderly Americans cam-cording the grounds break them up. People with shorts around their knees, acres of backside, and Yankees baseball hats pass them. Rob and Rox straighten up.

'Have a nice day, y'all,' Rob drawls, but the oldsters bumble past, threatened by his size and the scimitar tattoo in three colours on his forearm.

'I'll pick you up at half seven then,' Rob says.

He walks back to Milkwood, its web of chalets strung out on the hill in hopeful arrangement. Dreams float around in his head but he can't get at them. They seem forever out of his reach.

A Japanese family checks in at the office. Todd has gone into sales mode and pours over them like treacle. Rob catches Todd's eye and walks past with his most piss-taking walk, like John Wayne on a bad day.

It's always the same routine. Grass cutting, his nostrils stuffed with its green smell. Then comes the painting, the endless coating of wooden walls, which need constant protection against the salty sea air. Milkwood Timeshare. It was Sucksville for him and he had to get free of it.

Rob's mother was not around but the car was. It had a full tank too. At seven fifteen he was outside Roxie's, leaning on the horn. She took her time coming out, but it was worth the wait. She was poured into black leggings and a white top, her breasts like two firm fists trying to punch their way out. As she filled the car with her scent it was hard for Rob to keep calm.

'You're always early,' she says.

'I'm keen, 'an I?

Rob grins and guns the Ford, matching the revs to its pounding noise box. Bass bends the speakers and thumps like the ground is opening. They'll hear *him* coming.

'Jesus Christ, you're a crazy driver,' Roxie shouts, as Rob slips sideways around a bend, but she doesn't ask him to slow down. They are through Swansea's main in forty minutes and drinking on the Mumbles minutes after.

'Not gonna get pissed, are you?' Roxanne asks.

'Don' worry.'

Rob sweeps her up at the bar, crushes her to him, and runs hands over her. A sallow barman glares at them and wishes *he* was young again.

'Crazy,' Roxie whispers, biting Rob's ear.

They sit outside and drink lager the colour of the sunset.

The sun is going down on the bay, and gulls fool around above them, sending down screams like piercing bullets.

'It's like a big yolk, innit,' Rob says, nodding towards the setting sun.

'What?'

'Never mind. So when are we going off together?'

'Don' start that again. You're always skint.'

'More reason to go. How about London? There's lots of work there, even for barmaids.'

Rox scowls, pulls at her lower lip and looks about twelve years old. They smoke and eyeball the natives.

'This is where he was from,' she says.

'Who?'

'Dylan, your poet ponce. We done it in school. Ugly, lovely town, that's what he said 'bout Swansea.'

'He got it half right then. Thought that was the Manics anyway.' Rob downs his pint, and takes his boots off a chair. 'Les' go for a walk.'

'No way. Not tonight, I'm on.'

'Oh, that little scare over, is it?'

'I thought you'd never ask. Mr. Cool or what? What would you have done if I was?'

'What would *you* have done?'

'Sod.'

'I wouldn't stay in the village, I know that much.'

'Why didn't you do something in school then, instead of pissing about all the time?'

'Get real. You want to turn me into just another pen pusher? Busting a gut for someone else all my life?'

'Like you're doing now, you mean. Go on then. Surprise

me. What big idea do you have? Christ, you didn't even keep your music up.'

Rob jumps up, plays air guitar, turns it into a machine gun, and sprays the horizon. The sun is gone from it and Roxanne's question is not answered.

'Clown.'

'Come on, we're out of here.'

It's another race home, Roxanne praying that the police are not too active tonight, as Rob burns rubber. They get back in time to stop in the hotel for a few more drinks but stay at the bar, for the tables are full of outsiders. A mix of accents fills the air.

'Wankers,' Rob mutters, and not that quietly.

'Keep your voice down,' says Mrs. Judd, 'wankers they might be but they're my bread and butter. You look nice, Roxie, love. I had a figure like yours once.'

'I've applied for a job,' Rox says.

'You what?' Rob asks, waiting away his frothy moustache.

'Another job. In a bookshop in Carmarthen.'

Derision rises up in Rob, followed by rage and then jealousy. They are the spiteful seas on which he sails.

'Don' be so fuckin' stupid. You? In a bookshop?'

'I've got an interview. Tomorrow.' She laughs and digs him in the ribs. 'So *I'll* be the one out of the village.'

Fists clench, drink spills. Roxie enjoys his reaction but is scared. Mrs. Judd looks on, eagle-eyed, defensive. The tourists are wary at the modest commotion and Mrs. Judd scowls. 'Baby boy having a little tantrum, is he?' she says quietly, turning to smile at her seated clients

More white-knuckle anger. Rob hates surprises if they aren't his.

'If you can't behave,' Mrs. Judd says.

'He'll be all right,' Rox says.

Rob fights for control. Red begins to fade to boredom again, that grey limbo he seems to live in these days.

'It's thirty pound more than here,' Rox says. 'Know what I'd like to do, start something here one day, with books and stuff, and food. No one seems to mix the two. When I learn the business like.'

'You have been thinking, haven't you? Gonna get this job then, are you?'

'Why not? They wanted four G.C.S.E.s. I've got five.'

Take her home, get rat-arsed, get away, Rob's inner tongue clucks, but he is feeling the drink. It's starting to clog up his thoughts. They leave.

'Haven't seen you reading no books,' Rob mutters outside Roxie's house.

'I *have*. It's what people want, the ones that come here.'

Rob leaves Roxanne quite suddenly.

'You can help Mrs Judd clear up,' he says, over his shoulder. It seems to him a classy way to have the last word. He parks up the car, and walks off when his old girl rushes to the door, standing like a witch in a pool of yellow light, screaming about her car. He walks down to the front to eyeball the stars, which are like bright shining pins tonight. The castle looms dark as he passes it, and sea wet-slaps the rocks. Maybe he does love this place but it changes nothing.

Roxanne gets the job, Rob gets more chalets to paint, and Todd is still a growth on his back. He's pissed off with everyone. Roxie getting into heritage, culture, and other stuff he doesn't understand, but he knows they are words that go backwards in search of money. He knows it won't work, not for her; she is out of her depth, her class. It is a dream, her dream. At least his are big.

A few weeks later and Rob is stalking Roxanne in Carmarthen. He sees her leaving the shop, Book Paradise. The name almost makes him puke. She's dressed different, not so much colour, or leg. Wannabee clothes. They'd rucked bad since she started the job. Fists got the better of him at the weekend. Shocking them both. Roxie finished with him and did not change her mind five minutes later.

She clocks him coming up behind her and tries to walk quicker but he's alongside.

'Get lost, Rob. We're over.'

'Come to London with me.'

'So you can knock me around some more? I like it here. Without you.'

He takes her arm, but she shakes him off. There's a cop on the other side of street.

'I'll call him if you don't piss off,' Roxie says. '*You* go to London. Be a star or something. Follow your bloody mouth.'

His fists want to go again but he manages to fight them down, and his pride with them.

'I won't do it again,' Rob mutters.

'Oh aye. That's what they all say. I don' wanna know. And you're banned from the hotel, Mrs. Judd said.'

Get in front of her, make her look at me, Rob thinks. He

does but its no go. Her eyes blank him, she doesn't even say anything about his new haircut. The cop crosses the road. Fuck it. Rob leaves her and turns down an alley, back to the car he shouldn't be driving.

He's there when Roxanne gets off the bus. Rob feels like he does when he watches the visitors in their flash cars, flash clothes and plummy kids, watches them in his sweat-stained overalls when they check into Milkwood. Weighing up his weekly pittance against their fat lives.

'Not you again,' Roxie says.

She is more confident. He's the one who wants. Needs. She stops and turns to face him. Be cool, Rob, be cool.

'You just won't accept it, will you? Mrs. Judd says that when a fella starts using his fists he never stops.'

Rob sees the hotel going up in flames, Mrs. Judd burning in hell-fire. *Be cool.*

'I been going through a bad patch,' Rob says. 'Fed up, like.'

'You've always been going through a bad patch. You expect everything to fall into your hands. For you just to *have*. Like magic.'

They walk and she does not tell him to go.

'Gimme one more chance.'

'Why should I?'

Don't touch her, keep your hands down.

'Cos I... wan' one'

'You? Mr. Cool?'

'Yeah.'

He dares a hand now, on her arm, hesitant as a leaf then

118

pressing a bit firmer. *Almost there now.* Roxie turns her head close to his.

'You better mean it, Rob. If you ever do it again, that's it. You won't even exist for me.'

Heads flying, they grab at each other in relief.

'Les' go straight to the hotel,' Rob says, 'Mrs. Judd will serve me, if you sweet-talk her. I'll pay.'

Three hours later they are both falling down pissed as they leave the pub. There's still some red light streaking the sky, but the sea is a flat, grey lid. Apart from them, all is still in the village. They stagger along the front and collapse into a seat near that poet's place.

'We're great together, in' we?' Rob shouts, 'fuckin' great.'

There's no one else about to tell so he shouts it at the sky. Roxie giggles and clings onto him.

'We're gonna go up to London and do something. You'll see.'

Rob is swept along on his own words and Mrs. Judd's lager. With an effort he pushes himself up. He leans over the wall, and looks down at the Boathouse.

'I'm gonna climb that fucker. Sit on top of our poxy money-maker.'

He's over the gate before Roxie knows what's happening.

Rob slips again, fear sobering him up fast, booze drying out his mouth until it sucks on empty. He tastes bitter iron. But it's not just fear, it's exhilaration. That he is doing something, but not really sure what it is, what has taken hold of him.

He smells the sea, its salty waste, as he nears the roof.

Snaking his way up the pipe, hanging onto guttering that threatens to give way but holds. He's there, crouching gingerly on its mossy grease, until he can manage to raise himself up into the wind. Exhilaration turning to elation as he shouts out and pounds the air like a miniature King Kong. He bays at the moon and stars. He's as mad as a loon, and just as happy. Rob is a mad, happy, baying loon. He's on top of the world, a wild Celt taunting powerful demons, and delaying the inevitable with a false sense of triumph.

IN THE WAKE OF THE SUN

Eduardo watched the sun go down as he waited for the young man to come. Robbed of most of its strength, he thought how like an eye it was, shot through with blood and fire. An eye to serve for all those he had seen at the point of death. Like that priest's eye, disbelief locked in it forever when his moment came. He could still see his face clearly, more clearly than his old sight could make out the sun's last display, the way it red-streaked the sky, and played its final shafts across the dusty plain.

Maria served Eduardo coffee.

'He is late, your visitor,' she said.

'We can allow it,' Eduardo answered, 'he's been looking for me for a long time.'

'Not so long,' Maria said, 'he is young, just starting out in life.'

Eduardo smiled at his housekeeper of thirty years. He saw how age had marked her, the lines splayed all over her face a sign of her long years in the sun. Maria's long hair was piled up high on her head these days, like a web of spun silver.

Eduardo sipped his coffee whilst he waited, and added another sugar behind Maria's back. He shivered a little. It was late October, and getting chilly in the wake of the sun. Eduardo noticed it more with each passing year. He played with one of the scars on his arm as sixty-year old visions became clear again. This day his visitor might make them even more vivid.

Maria saw him first, from her kitchen window. He was a tall man, with a shock of black hair, looking at the wrought iron numbers on the doors of houses as he strode with purpose down the shadowy street. Maria ushered their guest into the main room. He stood awkwardly amongst the heavy, ancient furnishings and faded paintings. He'd expected the place to shout out its military past, to be a witness to the colonel's life, but only one blurred image of a young officer was in evidence, framed in silver on a table.

'Father Felippe,' Eduardo said, as he entered the room. 'I am sorry to have kept you waiting.'

Eduardo spread his hands in apology as each man studied the other. Enquiring eyes of a striking blue went well with the priest's dark hair. Eduardo suppressed a sigh. Perhaps it was a mistake to see this young man, to go over such old days. Others had come, when Franco died and the country began to change. But they were after history, facts, nothing so personal as this one.

Maria brought in more coffee and a plate of small, dry biscuits. Eduardo gestured the priest to a chair and sat down himself.

'There is a chill in the evening air,' Eduardo said.

Felippe nodded. So far he was a man of few words, but Eduardo could feel his determination. He saw it in his steadfast eyes, and knew it had been fuelled by the long telling of the past that must have taken place in his family. Each year their version of history would take on more weight, and become blinded with righteousness. His own side had been masters at it. What research the young man must have done, to track him down from one solitary death amongst the hundreds he had witnessed, amongst the million that took place.

'So, you are a Catalan,' Eduardo said. 'I have never been there, not even to Barcelona. Ask your questions, father.'

There was a silence. The bell of a church could be heard, a rather plaintive marking of time that rang out into the dying of the day. Eduardo had not noticed the folder the priest was carrying at first, for its black cover merged with his vestments. *Con permiso,* the priest said, but he did not wait for it as he opened the folder on the table, then stood behind it, expectantly.

'How old are you?' Eduardo asked.

'Twenty-five.'

Eduardo nodded. Older by some years than he'd been when Franco flew in from Africa to save civilisation, as he put it. He was a rotund, showy little man, none too bright either, but dangerous, because he was too stupid to be anything else. Eduardo had never come under that man's sway or suffered his favour, and he was glad of that.

Felippe began to talk. 'My grandfather's brother was the first priest in our family. Father Luiz. You do remember him, don't you? In Málaga? You would not have seen me otherwise.'

'You were persistent, father, determined, but I like that. The ability to keep at something is a quality I prize in myself.'

Eduardo enjoyed this small vanity and realised he had no one to talk any more. No longer the animated conversations of his youth and middle years, talk shot through with politics and religion – the very stuff of Spain. All the people worth talking to were dead. Now it was just the day-to-day running of the house with Maria. Sometimes she prattled on about her over-large family and its problems, but he usually let her words flow over him like poorly aimed bullets.

'Málaga,' Eduardo said, 'I was not there long.'

'Long enough,' said Felippe.

'Ah, you have it all there, I suppose,' Eduardo said.

'I have made a chart of your part in the war, yes.'

Eduardo smiled. A *chart*. Such an intrusion would have infuriated him once. Now he savoured its irony, violent and instinctive action from another age being evaluated with the hindsight of half a century.

'You think I am a monster?' Eduardo said.

Felippe kept his eyes on his folder. His face answered for him. Eduardo caught his own in the window, as the last light filled the room. This was his favourite time of day. The sun beneath the horizon diffused into an orange glow and this light softened his worn features and smoothed out the crevices of his brow.

'If I am such,' Eduardo said, 'how does that serve you? My time is almost over. *My* Spain certainly is. So what do you want from me? What are you looking for?'

'I am trying to understand my family's past. This country's past.'

'That's a lot to understand.'

'And I want to come to terms with our country's barbarism. We are almost in a new millennium now, and maybe a new age.'

'Just as well you are not German,' Eduardo muttered.

He was tired, and would have preferred this interview earlier in the day.

'When I received your first letter I did not remember that priest,' Eduardo said, 'not at first. It was in the early days of the war, when everything seemed to explode. I had not long received my commission. The priest had taken part in the fighting, taking pot shots at us from his bell tower. A captain had been killed. His execution was inevitable.'

'And if he had been a common soldier?'

'Probably the same. Neither side was overly concerned with prisoners. Civil war is decidedly uncivil, no? And the priest's action was viewed as a form of treachery, especially as the clergy, by and large, favoured our side. The socialists, communists, whatever you want to call them, killed many more of them than us. I remember the remains of nuns they dug up being hung outside cathedrals.'

'I am aware of this,' Felippe said, as he thumbed through his file. 'It was late September. The weather like it is today. The firing squad was not a success. You finished his life.'

'An officer's job.'

'I found one man from that squad last year. He has since died but he told me they all tried to miss.'

Eduardo shrugged, but he knew that man had lied.

'Very few families are untouched by a civil war. It is a family affair, and families are like volcanoes, they can erupt at any time, spilling out all their bile on the unsuspecting.'

Maria re-entered the room. Did they want more coffee? Perhaps some wine? She was reverential around the young priest, thrilled by Felippe's visit. Before she left, Maria turned on the table lamp, and each man seemed trapped in its pool of yellow light. It seemed to bring them closer.

'We are coming to the end of a thousand years, you say?' Eduardo murmured. 'At my age I do not find that particularly exciting, though I am surprised to still be here to witness it. I am eighty-four years old – but you know that. You must know many things about me that I have forgotten. That I no longer want to know.'

They were silent again for a time. The town was waking up again, and people were thinking of food and company as they stepped out. The sounds of the street, the footsteps and the conversation, were those which encouraged Eduardo's loneliness.

'Do you want me to apologise,' he said, 'for all my ancient violence? For doing the same as so many others? My conscience is clear, and so are my dreams.'

He was lying to this young priest. His dreams were not so comfortable, and never had been. Some nights, violent images ripped through his mind, many of them curiously washed of colour, like old newsreels. Maybe this was what the priest wanted, to check if guilt weighed him down, and then to tease it out of him. Eduardo was not a religious man and confession had been the only benefit of the church when he was young, the instant relief of blaming oneself before anyone else could. But he had nothing to confess now, only the numbing boredom of his twilight years.

'I ask you again, Father Felippe, what do you want of me? I have seen you. Here I am, so what's the point of all this?'

Father Luiz had kept a journal, which was now in Felippe's possession. It contained his thoughts on the

126

country in the thirties, on the Republic and the part his church played in its downfall. Each page told of his unease and doubt, then his dismay at the unchanging ways of his faith, at its cruel blindness to the plight of Spain's poor. Felippe knew it had caused his death because it had caused him to fight, to rebel against his calling. The likes of the Colonel had seen to that, and they had kept the country locked up with old ways for another forty years. Yet how urbane the old man seemed, and he still had the vanity to dye his thin moustache.

He wonders at me, Eduardo thought. At all those I might have killed and caused to be killed. He is still young, young enough to expect evil to appear in the face. If I was evil. They followed ideologies worlds apart but there was something in Felippe that he liked, a stubborn honesty perhaps, certainly a doggedness to follow a trail that led to him. His part in the death of an old adversary had been confirmed, but that was all. It was one small blip in his bloody past.

'You are the last living link, *señor*, with these words.' Felippe said, tapping his file. 'You have shaped my family, played a part in the way it has evolved.'

Eduardo raised an eyebrow.

'No children would have ensued, I left no woman widowed.'

'No, but my grandfather was greatly affected by his brother's death. He was on your side, you know, but he took the family away from Spain, to Montpelier. I am as much French as Spanish. We remained in exile for a generation. When I became a priest I chose to return.'

You shouldn't have, Eduardo thought. Always go forward. Never back.

'Does it really matter any more?' Eduardo said. 'The republic is back, socialists, so called, are back. I doubt there will ever be another Franco. Spain is too sophisticated for beliefs of that sort now. It has television.'

The table lamp was getting stronger, as daylight faded. Eduardo could hold out no longer. He rang for Maria and told her to bring in sherry. It was long overdue. Felippe declined to join him, so Eduardo got up and stood by the window, one hand behind his back, the other moving the glass around, letting its pale honey-coloured liquid catch the table light.

'So,' Eduardo asked, 'when will you go back?'

'I have a train in the morning.'

'A civilised way to travel.'

We are both discomforted by this anti-climax, Eduardo thought. In another time, another age, with another man, I might have expected assassination, the end of a blood feud. But we have no feud, just a shared history. Something has come to an end this night for Felippe, but he is not fulfilled. He will always be a searcher after illusory truths. That is his cross to bear.

'To travel across Spain for such a short time with me, is that really worthwhile to you?' Eduardo said.

'Oh yes, to see you was vital.'

'The Republic of '36 could never have worked, you know. Not then. There was no reality to it. But when Franco died Spain was ready.'

'We will never agree on that, Colonel.'

Eduardo raised his glass.

'Perhaps not, but at least we are not fighting. Is that not progress?'

Felippe readied himself to go. 'I will leave this with you,' he said, tapping the file. 'I made a copy.'

He got up quickly, quick enough to startle Eduardo. A few drops of sherry spilled from the glass. He smiled in embarrassment, but the priest seemed not to notice.

Eduardo offered the priest his hand, expecting it to be ignored, but Felippe took it. He felt the charge from a hand sixty years younger than his, its strength in the loose folds of his own. But he matched the firmness of the shake.

Felippe closed his folder and asked his last question. 'Do you remember what Luiz said, at the end?'

'He was very calm. That is all I can say.'

'Thank you, Colonel Martinez.'

Maria appeared in the doorway and she fussed the young priest out without another word. Eduardo stepped onto the balcony to watch him go. Felippe did not look back or hesitate as he walked away along a street which was now almost in darkness. His austere guest was too much in control for that, Eduardo thought. Perhaps his predecessor Luiz had been of similar temperament, before the fighting started.

Maria was putting away the sherry as Eduardo went back inside. He stopped her.

'Tonight I want more,' he murmured.

Maria was in a good mood, still excited. She glanced at Eduardo, dreaming that he would recant his Godless past. He waved her away and sat at his desk with the priest's folder. He turned its pages hesitantly. Memories raced through his head, and they were all as sharp as knives. He could even smell the past now. The many deaths that littered it, the women, the hopes shrivelled, renewed, and shrivelled again. The rapidity of it all. And he could see that priest. He had not been calm at all, and had begged for his life like a child. He'd even cursed his God.

'Are you all right, Colonel?' Maria said.

Eduardo nodded. He thought she had already left the room.

'Did the meeting go well? Father Felippe seemed very nice. So clean cut. Not like the young men of my family.'

'Cleanliness and godliness, eh, in one visit. Do you want to join me for a glass of this fine Amontillado, Maria?'

'Colonel, that is not right. You have never said anything like that to me in all our years together.'

'To celebrate the presence of God?'

He poured out a small glass for her. Maria stared at him.

'Take the glass, Maria. Drink with me this one time.'

She did as he said, wasting the sherry in one nervous gulp. This time Maria did leave him, alone with his thoughts and the priest's chart. He imagined her tongue flapping the next morning. By then she'd have him down as either a converted heretic or a silly old fool. Perhaps both.

He could smell that morning in Málaga. Taste the crisp autumn air displacing the legacy of a heavy summer, and winning. He had worried then that the fighting would be over too soon. His whole being was suffused in the art of killing, and the concentration it took to stay alive. Savouring every minute of it.

A sudden yearning to have that feeling again came upon

Eduardo with a passion. He turned the silver framed photograph to face him and looked at himself with the years stripped away. He doubted that his life had been good but it had been full. It was a tight-fitting uniform and his pistol stood out proudly. He still had it, locked in a draw in the desk. It took him a while to find the key.

The gun had lain there for many years with its small box of bullets. Its timeless presence filled the room as he polished it. Eduardo inserted the brass-capped charges into the cylinder and rotated it, a fascinated child still.

His health had always been good. He knew he would reach the next millennium and get some years into it but suddenly the thought appalled him. The past had piled up into unmanageable quantities, leaving only ennui and regret, and it lay like a lead weight on his soul. Father Felippe had drawn the final line under it, whether he'd planned to or not. Eduardo was so tired.

He finished the sherry and turned off the lamp. A last afterglow of the sunset settled into the room as he smoothed down his hair and straightened his jacket.

Maria thought a car in the street caused that sharp crack. Boys often rushed up and down in their fast machines. An hour later she brought in Eduardo's nightcap, a pot of China tea. The tray spilled to the floor as she stifled a scream with her hand. The Colonel could not abide that sort of emotion.

THE BATTLE OF CULLODEN

Duncan squashes a midge in the hairs of his forearm, and flicks the remnants into the breeze. It's a brief moment of power that helps clear his head. He notices a darker blood mixing with bright red and gives his arm a suck, tasting iron through the bristles of his moustache. Sitting up in the heather, he sniffs the air like a seal, and then stands up stiffly. He leans against a flag post and shakes dew and cramp from his joints. Dawn is seeping in through brightening cloud cover as sleep reluctantly drops from Duncan's bleary eyes.

Under the yellow flag at the centre of the killing fields Duncan turns to face each direction in turn. To the south west, mountains rear up their soft, misty bulges. Elsewhere all is flat. Low ground, low vegetation, and pink-lilac heather shading scrubby gorse, which is tough and springy, like his beard. The heather was his mattress for the night.

Duncan runs a hand through the crust of his hair, and wipes his nose on a sleeve. It is too early for tourists to be disgorged from buses and cars, or the fat motor homes that snail the highland roads. From his den he watched these arrive the day before. Loud Yanks in sportswear that mocked their age, Germans with large bags strapped across larger rears and Japanese, always them, moving in smiling, puzzled unity. All prodding at his past with their ignorant tongues.

A crow floating low notes his presence, and marks it with a cry that cuts the silence. It wheels away as Duncan turns his arm into a rifle. Wise bird, he mutters. Light increases and his head improves. Back comes the feeling of the night, before he got too far into the bottle.

His eyes flit around the landscape. This place, he thinks, this awesome bloody place. It was said that it has not changed since the battle and Duncan believes it. No one can live here, or build here. It has too much grip on the nation's soul; too much pain, guilt, and heinous pride is bled into every fold in the ground. When he traces the names of the clans on the small plaques Duncan feels the ground opening up its wound, offering it to him, encouraging him with its bitterness. For twenty years he has spoon-fed himself on its myth, until it comes to justify his whole sad being

Twenty years of snatching at history from his vacuum of ignorance. Before, he had known only the tenements. *They* were his history. Booze, beatings, dubious parentage, addled treatment, the past a jumble of whisky-soaked words spurted out in incoherent torrents by wasted associates.

To get the knowledge he had to break away. Working summers on the land, serving the tourists that mingled with the deer in the emptied highlands, using his eyes and ears as he stalked museums and libraries, even though their books defeated him. Words had always jammed in his head as a kid; anger always defeated meaning as he traced them with dirty fingers. The whole fucking system had jammed in his head. Drunks had charted his real learning, when he stood on the fringes in pubs, and misunderstood the talk of educated folk.

Now Duncan is here at the burning heart of his Scotland.

Talk had so often centred on Culloden. At first he had thought it a man, then, over the years, words had taken shape, and he gained a semblance of understanding. Then Duncan saw an old film at an arts centre he conned his way into, and the words were fleshed out with pictures, which he'd flash through his head to stoke his lonely anger. This became his daily movie.

Duncan sinks back down into his sleeping bag. Rolling a thin cigarette, he lies back and looks at the grey canopy above him, waiting for the museum and shop to open, his eyes slits in his ruined face. He enjoys spitting out the odd strands of tobacco that stick in his teeth.

It is ten past nine. Mavis works on her nails with a small file, curving them into a symmetry that pleases her. Ann, a much younger and smaller woman, checks the float in the till.

'We need silver,' she says, already bored with the day.

Mavis does not look up from her nails.

'We'll be all right. If you run short Jamie's always got plenty.'

Mavis finished the last nail and reached for her lacquer.

'Looks like rain,' Ann says.

Jamie waves from his gift shop. Mavis likes to see him first thing in the morning. His tall, kilted figure reminds her of her husband thirty years ago. Dead for ten years now. She sighs, and tells Ann to give the counter a clean.

'Then get us a cuppa,' she says, 'before the invasion starts.'

The centre is quite new. Not long ago Mavis walked this edge of the moor with her dog. Now enterprise has made something here and she has a job in late middle age. She mans the museum till with Ann, and fields the multifarious questions of visitors. Jamie runs the adjacent gift shop and a few young ones manage the cafe. It is work for them, but Mavis is glad she does not have to face a lifetime at the till. The place gives her the creeps sometimes. A few feet from her station are two life-sized figures in a glass display case. Bait to entice folk in. A highlander is engaging a redcoat, red-splashed claymore against a bloodied bayonet on a long rifle, each figure in a wild-eyed killing frenzy. These are her other daily workmates.

Jamie sees Duncan first.

'Aw, Jesus, look what's coming in off the moor,' he says, as he stands drinking tea with the women.

Mavis glances through the entrance doors to see Duncan walking towards them. A ragged hirsute figure, slouching his way over the heather in a peculiar gait, battered rucksack on his shoulder.

'Good God,' she says, 'a tramp. I haven't seen one in years.'

'Well, he's no coming in here,' Jamie said. 'We'll have the punters arriving any minute.' He checks the folds of his kilt and straightens his matching tartan tie. 'He's been trespassing if he spent the night on the field. Shall I phone the police?'

'No, don't bother,' Mavis says. 'He's probably after a cup of tea. Take him round the back of the cafe, then send him on his way.'

Jamie steps outside to meet Duncan, who warms to the traditional figure appearing in front of him, his heart quickening at the sight of the tartan. Jamie looks over his shoulder and sees the first car arriving. Kids tumble out of it, English accents approach, in shorts.

'Can I help you, pal?' Jamie asks Duncan.

'Wassat?'

Duncan rubs a hand across his parched mouth, scratches under an arm and hitches up his rancid jeans. The English family pass them, Jamie standing in front of Duncan, as if to obliterate his presence.

'I been twenty years getting here, you ken?' Duncan says. 'Twenty fuckin' years.'

Jamie is not sure if the man is mad. His strange eyes seem to dart everywhere, bright pins of light in a florid, hairy face. Duncan lurches towards him in a friendly way and for one horrifying moment Jamie thinks he is about to be embraced. He smells piss and stale whisky on the old tramp. They should have security, he's always said so, being the only man on site. Behind him the till begins to chatter as Mavis admits the family.

'Our history, right,' Duncan says, waving a hand expansively. 'What a feeling, eh, out on the moor. I woke up with my guts full of it. Bastard English.'

The first bus arrives. Jamie knows it by its livery; it brought Americans on the highland tour.

'You've been trespassing, pal,' Jamie says, 'on Trust land. Look, come round the back, get a cup of tea. Then you can be on your way.'

'That's a fine wee kilt, son. What clan might that be?'

The Americans are advancing, mainly plump geriatrics in

tracksuit-like gear. They stop for a moment to admire Jamie, and get close enough to smell Duncan.

'Jeez, that guy stinks,' one says.

'Maybe he's part of the show, huh?'

'Looks like a bum to me.'

Duncan tries to line himself up with the Americans but Jamie stops him.

'Wassamarra? I can no come in? It's been twenty years. I got money.'

He flourishes a crumpled fiver in front of Jamie's face. Jamie feels the eyes of a semi-circle of tourists on him.

'Won't let him in, huh?'

'That guy's a mess. Like a wino or something.'

'What's he doing here, anyway?'

'Henry, don't you go near that man.'

'Please go inside, folks,' Jamie says.

The aftermath of the whisky wells up in Duncan. Waves of nausea lap up inside him and behind them comes the desire for more drink. He wants to piss too. What was this young fella up to? Stopping *him*, Duncan MacLeish, from coming in.

'Keep an eye on the shop for me,' Jamie shouts to a staring Ann. She stands in the doorway, enthralled by this change in her dull routine as Jamie leads away a stumpy man, all red hair and stink.

'Aye, I camped out in the field,' Duncan says, as Jamie propels him along. 'On that ground of blood.'

He stretches his face up to Jamie's. The air turns fetid.

'Jesus Christ,' Jamie mutters.

'He's no here, son, he never was. Bastard English, eh?'

'Don't you ever wash?' Jamie says.

137

He manages to sit Duncan on the chair that's always outside by the kitchen's back door. They are out of sight at last.

'Now, you're not going to cause trouble, are you? You've already trespassed.'

'Private, like, is it?'

'I'll get you some tea, and then you have to be off.'

'Aye aye, son. Aye aye.'

Jamie feels infested as he enters the kitchen. Different parts of his body prickle.

'That your boyfriend you got there, Jamie lad?' asks Jody, the kitchen help.

'Don't you start. He's some old tramp, up from Glasgow by the sound of him. Stinks like old fish. Give us a mug of tea.'

'He looks harmless enough. Not much bigger than me.' Jody hands Jamie the tea, and, as an after thought, a slab of stale cake she is about to bin. 'Stick a beret on him and he could pass for one of those exhibits in the museum.'

'I've got to get back to the shop,' Jamie says. 'Keep an eye on him will you?'

'Oh, ta very much.'

Jamie thrusts the tea and cake into Duncan's hands.

'*Don't* come to the front of the building. I'll have to call the police if you do'

'You got it, captain.'

Duncan wraps his well-worn cloak of subservience about him. He can wait. He sinks small pieces of cake into the tea, letting it dissolve into a soggy mass, which he sucks through the remnants of his teeth. After breakfast he'll have a look inside. All that earwigged chat of the last twenty years will come to life there, come to life for him.

Jamie is back at his counter. His girl has phoned in sick, just what he needs. Some visitors come straight into the shop, others walk out into the fields first. It's a good set up – fire up imaginations with vivid history, then follow up with gifts to celebrate their visit, and instant knowledge, especially those looking for scraps of a Scottish past. A lot of what he sells is third world tat but it provides a good living, even if he does sometimes feel a prat having to wear the kilt. As his till begins to sing Jamie forgets about Duncan, who is inside and past Mavis before anyone knows it, lost in the midst of more bus loads.

It takes a minute for Duncan's eyes to adjust to the subdued lighting. The museum is a small place. A few rooms with exhibits under glass, or the past lived out in life-sized corners. Lots of things Duncan cannot read. He keeps one eye on the entrance and the other on the weapons. His hand fits into the wire cage of a broadsword. He has dirks about his person, a flintlock pistol in his belt and heather on his beret as dreams catch fire, and his heart melts to the pipes. He sidles up to tourists until their noses are alerted to him and they part like the sea before Moses.

It's hard for Duncan to breathe, such is his excitement. This was his people's last stand. All around him they cry as they spill their lives, and lives were something to spill then, not like the grey existence that is his own. And honour was alive in the land, something worth having, and worth dying for.

Duncan ducks behind a display when he sees Jamie enter the museum, but is cornered easily as the place empties.

'You stupid old bugger,' Jamie shouts. 'What did I tell you? Come on, let's have you out of here.'

Duncan charges him, head down into the stomach. Jamie is knocked to the floor. His kilt flares and red underwear is flashed in Duncan's face. Duncan runs out onto Culloden field, snuffling low over the ground like some strange animal. He tries to burrow into the gorse, but it is not high enough for cover so he sits up, startling an American couple that are passing.

'Arright,' Duncan says, face curving into a bashful smile.

'What are you doing there, fella?' the American asked.

His wife touches his arm.

'Henry, you be careful. That's the one who was outside the museum.'

'Arright,' Duncan repeats. He shakes bits of green from his person, though they seem to belong there. 'What a place, eh? Been twenty years.'

'Twenty years?' Henry asks, ignoring his wife.

'Aye, getting here, like. This is everything for me. My birthright. My soul.'

'He's gaga,' mutters Henry's wife. She holds her handbag against her, like armour.

'Go join the others dear,' Henry says, 'I want to talk to this guy.'

'I would have thought you'd had enough by now. *History*. Ford was right about it.'

'Wee hen getting you down, pal?' Duncan says, 'ach, they all do that. Words like arrows, mouths like whales.'

Henry waits until his wife is out of range.

'I'm Cullis, Henry Cullis, retired history professor. British history, actually.'

Henry thinks better of offering a hand. He just waves one and Duncan copies him.

'Duncan MacLeish, Scotsman. British history, eh? Does that include Scottish history?'

'Of course, that's why we're here.'

'Know a lot about Culloden?'

Henry sits his long frame upwind of Duncan. He notices other walkers veering away from them.

'I guess so. How about you?'

'I know everything about it. I've lived and breathed it for twenty years. Bastard English.'

'Huh huh. Mildred's folks came over to the States at the time of the clearances. I've some Irish too, way back.'

'That right?'

Duncan flicks his eyes around but no one is coming for him. He wonders what clearances were too.

'Why do you say *bastard English*?' Henry asks.

'They destroyed us back then, the flower of the Highlands. Bonnie Scots, one and all.'

Henry thinks he has Duncan pegged right. A pint-sized man with an I.Q. to match, juggling with fragments of half-truths. A little knowledge blended with a lot of myth. It's not his business, but he can't help himself. He wants to shoot Duncan down. Mildred has pissed him off in the eight days they've been in Scotland, her words as bleak and penetrating as the weather. They should have had kids.

Duncan crouches in his bush. Henry thinks he might be

deranged but he does seem to belong here. He is like living history springing up through a fold in the ground. A wild man for a wild place. This Duncan guy would have fitted in well in that French fop's army. Ill-led, ill-fed, people hopelessly and blindly ending a way of life.

'Actually there were more Scots than English in the Royalist army,' Henry says bluntly. 'Lowlanders with scores to settle, mainly – Mildred's ancestry. And some Northern Irish, Welsh, Hanoverian mercenaries, you name it. Less than half were English.'

The words float around Duncan for a while, and then penetrate.

'Ach, you're joking me. You Yanks, eh?'

'It's true. Absolutely.'

'You're fucking mental, Johnny. I been around, I heard everything about Culloden. It's taken me—'

'Twenty years. Yeah, I know that part. Haven't you ever read any books on the subject?'

Looking closely at Duncan, Henry regrets his question. He's getting to be too grouchy, and feels a little guilty. Duncan's eyes smoulder in his small, hairy head. Whisky-shot orbs set well back.

'The Redcoats behaved appallingly after the battle, it's true,' Henry says, in a milder tone, suddenly aware of his aloneness with this man. His hands clasp his walking stick.

Duncan rocks quietly on his haunches, keening to the wind. Henry sweeps his eyes about the field, at its feral, wind-straggled contours, made strange by the soft yellows and pinks of vegetation. This old wino was right about one thing, this place was goddam eerie.

'Highland life was not idyllic at all,' Henry continues, getting into his old lecturing mode,' it was more like barbaric, a feudal system out of the dark ages. People were enslaved by it.'

Over Duncan's shoulder Henry sees a police car arriving at the centre, and uniformed figures talking to that young man in the kilt. They are being pointed his way.

Duncan's head seethes. This old Yank is a loony. Professor, be buggered. God, he feels rough. He can't remember eating yesterday, and now his guts churn and thrash as he farts and belches simultaneously. It's a speciality of his. His tongue snakes out like a piece of pink meat and sucks at the hair around his mouth. Someone is shouting, or is that just the wind carrying a voice from the past? He often hears them. A hand clamps on his shoulder.

'Having fun, are we, pop?'

The policeman is big, burly and not so young himself.

'It's this one,' Duncan says, shaking his hair at Henry. 'Spouting crap about Culloden. About Scotland. Man's full of shite.'

Henry smiles.

The police exchange pitying glances as they catch Duncan's smell. He struggles as they carry him from the battlefield, his short legs pumping the air between the two officers. Henry walks behind, embarrassed. Tourists are grouping around the shop and Mildred's face like thunder is easy to pick out.

Duncan curves his head around for one last look, fixing the memory in his mind. Later he'll cement it in place with a few bottles and laugh at the daft Yank with his daft words.

The policemen push him through a curious crowd. He sees Jamie and winks. Duncan flashes his graveyard teeth as the first spits of rain begin to make hollows in his beard and shouts at his audience in a language they can barely recognise as English.

Mildred pulls Henry away. He feels the warmth of her angry hand as it tugs at his.

OFF THE SCRAPHEAP

Stones rained down onto the pile of wrecks, one managing to bounce off four metal hulks before it was spent. Harvey, jarred out of sleep, tottered on his chair, and almost fell, but the way he sprang up was instinctive. Arthritis was denied, stiffness ignored, and his tongue became young and supple.

'I know who you are,' Harvey shouted, 'I'll see your mothers.'

Once it had been fathers.

'Tosser,' the kids sang in unison, 'old man Harvey is a tosser.'

Three ten-year-olds stood on the slope behind the yard, laughing at him. He saw the gap-toothed grin of one catch the sun as few more stones came down. The screen of an old Vauxhall Viva shattered. He had almost forgotten it was in the yard. It has been there so long it was part of the ground now, a strange alliance of plant and metal, green growth thrusting through its holes and weed displays in the wounds of its headlights. The gap-toothed kid threw down another missile, but more hesitantly this time as Harvey approached them.

Then they were gone, snaking up the banking like eels on a land mission, laughing at their raid on his metal world. Harvey decided to close up early. Business was slow and a hot

August day was going nowhere. After padlocking the battered gates, he sat back down to enjoy the last of it and survey his business. Several hundred cars were wedged together, a steel sandwich of twisting, listing sculpture, all in various degrees of rusting, each one a burning russet as the afternoon sun came in low.

There was talk of a new road through Harvey's place. He had already been sounded out about it. It would mean real money, if he sold, or was made to sell. Harvey sighed and put this to the back of his mind. It was cash box time.

Opening the box never failed to put a thrill through his miser heart. Harvey loved the whole ritual. Turning the unwilling lock with a tarnished key, letting the lid squeak its way open, waiting for the light to fall onto the notes, especially the yellow light of a summer's evening. The way it saturated the violet twenties, and softened the features of each Faraday. He'd been a cash man all his life.

Each tin he had held two hundred twenties. The one he was currently filling was kept in the yard, in constantly changing hiding places. Recently it was in the glove compartment of a destroyed estate car. He'd been done over many times but they always looked in his tin shed office. His hiding places were open, but secret.

The tin was just about full. He could have crammed more notes into it but he liked the way two hundred notes settled into the space and the symmetry of the notes was pleasing. It was easy to flick through them with a moist thumb, to enjoy their satisfying feel, some notes crisp and clean, others limp and dirty. He was on his tenth tin. That made forty thousand quid, tax-free. Not bad for someone who had the chance of another hundred grand from the council if the road went ahead. Harvey put the tin in a supermarket bag and made his way home.

The road to the yard was a wonderful disgrace, with deep potholes capable of busting any axle. Harvey liked it that way. He was getting to be a wreck himself, with a face like the pocked bonnet of an old Ford, and hands calloused as his walking stick. He was bus pass age but still had some fire left. There was a touch of defiance about the eyes, which were still bright and lively.

Harvey walked across the river bridge that led from the yard and glanced down into the swirling waters. They were clean green over a brown bed, as a century of coal dust had been eradicated in just ten years. Those stone throwing kids had never seen it dirty. Even so the past was not so easily gone. A twirl of orange seeped out from a banking as old iron workings found their way to the river. He watched swifts dive-bomb clouds of gnats like demented Spitfires. They always seemed to congregate over this part of the river, as if the colour orange was driving them mad. Swifts were getting rare these days.

Lorna Edwards was approaching. Her old man had worked with him underground and had copped it in a fall. Harvey had been pulled clear and Lorna had never forgiven him. He'd got out after that, out and up into the air, the diesel-tainted air of the scrap yard, which he'd bought with his pay-off money.

'All right?' Harvey muttered as they passed.

Lorna sniffed in return, and for a moment he thought their sticks might fight. Christ, he hated being old. Hated the way his body no longer kept pace with his thoughts. Despite himself, Harvey glanced back, knowing that she would do the same. He knew she was remembering that time in Porthcawl, the miner's fortnight in '53 when he'd tried to screw a year in Korea out of his system. Harvey was remembering too; he saw Ava, Lorna's best friend, who had become his girl.

Harvey's eyes softened as he mouthed her name. Ava, it was an exotic name for those days. Memories flitted through his head. More than four decades slipped away easily to reveal his youth, lust, hope, and his gleaming, broad-backed health. He saw Ava's receptive body and ebony hair and his pursuit of her for most of that year on the back of lies and bullshit. Then losing her, on the back of lies and bullshit. Letting loss fester inside him until it became the reason for his attitude, the excuse for his selfishness. No one else ever came close. He'd aged quickly, it seemed to him now, racing on and away from that one chance of happiness. Harvey was so lost in his thoughts he didn't realise that Lorna had turned back.

'Miles away, aren't you,' Lorna said, rapping on the ground with her stick, 'silly old fool.'

Harvey scowled, and thrust his hands around his own stick.

'Spend too much time in that junkyard, you do, though maybe it's the best place for you.'

'How's that boy of yours? Haven't seen him driving around lately.'

'He's working away. He's got a *decent* car, now.'

'Good. Been a nice day, hasn't it?'

'Trying to be friendly doesn't suit you, Dick.'

Harvey shrugged and made to go.

'You've heard about Ava's husband, I suppose,' Lorna said.

'You suppose wrong.'

'She wrote to me a few weeks ago. Her Ken died, six months ago.'

'Oh.'

Did she ask about me, Harvey wanted to ask, did she ask about me, but he kept his mouth shut.

'I'll see you then,' he said.

Harvey remembered Ken all right, he remembered the shock of losing out to him only too well. That was a kipper in the face of his ego all those years ago. It still was. Ava had moved to the next valley, then down to the softer Vale as Ken's star rose. He'd kept tabs on her for a while, kept the wound open.

Harvey walked on to his house and put the filled tin with the others, in the *safe* he had made in the kitchen, a hole on the wall behind the gas boiler, where his loot could be kept nice and warm. He could be near it whilst he sat at the table. Harvey's was the last terrace in the village, listing a little crazily now, like himself.

It had been a fine spell of weather, evening skies saturated with red and orange, and air heavy with the day's heat. From his kitchen window Harvey could see right down the valley, follow its sweep to the grey blob of the sea with his eyes. He knew every fold of it, but neither hated nor loved it.

That night Harvey's old thoughts refused to let him alone.

He went to bed with images of Ava as a twenty year old. Like Ava Gardner, he thought, only better.

The sun held, burning down onto Harvey's junk empire with an intensity he had not known in recent years. Business slowed to a trickle of impoverished banger drivers in search of cheap parts. He began to shut up early, mid-afternoons, and walk back the long way, along the riverbank and over the ornate Victorian iron bridge. It had been recently done up by the council, regaining much of its pomp, but now looking out of place. He was living in a period of change, but it was the past that held his thoughts. Ava's face was apt to break in on him any time, eyes shining, hair sleek and black, and a gypsy-like complexion. He told himself to cut it out, but Ava would not go away. She nestled in his mind, his lost bird of paradise.

Harvey was sitting on the riverbank when Lorna approached him, sticking her way across the iron bridge. Harvey hoped she was not coming his way, but she was, in a determined, uneven line.

'Thought it was you,' Lorna said.

'Twice in one year,' Harvey murmured. 'Almost a miracle'

'What's that?'

'Nothing.'

He slouched down on his elbows, waiting for her to go away.

'I've had another letter,' Lorna said.

'Oh aye.'

'From Ava. She's asked about you.'

His heart leapt. That stupid phrase from soppy fiction, yet it was the only way to describe it. His pulse raced as he tried not to appear interested, and his ticker went crazy in his sturdy chest, as if it was trying to fight its way out, trying to get some action at last.

'I phoned the number she gave me,' Lorna said. 'Told her about you, and the scrap yard – she laughed.'

'So, I've been discussed, have I?'

'Don't flatter yourself, you're not that important.'

Harvey slouched, and sank even lower down.

'Ava said she's coming over to see me. She's got a car. A *new* one. She learned to drive at sixty, she said.'

Lorna prodded her way carefully back over the bridge. She must have come looking for me, Harvey thought. He hadn't seen her this far from the house in years. What did it mean? The ticker started up again.

It was Sunday but Harvey still made his way to the yard. Its familiarity was usually a comfort, but something was missing today. Each wreck accused and mocked, and they spoke of all his lost years. In his tin shed he looked for and found a half bottle of whisky. He liked the occasional nip but this time he poured out a tumbler full, his eyes watering as it seared its way down. Maybe other things affected his eyes, for they were opening fully for the first time in forty years, and they saw Ava drive into the yard.

She drove through the gates in a Japanese car, a shining out-of-place jewel amongst his dross. He knew it was she instantly, and stood in front of the office self-consciously as Ava got out of the car. She was well turned out, and her legs still did it for him. He stood there in grease-daubed overalls, wondering where to put his hands. Why the hell had she come to the yard, he'd had no chance to prepare.

'Never thought I'd ever see you back here,' Harvey managed to say. 'It's been a long time.'

'I thought I'd give the old village a look over, but it hasn't changed much.'

'No. Nothing much to change.'

Cautiously, Ava probed the ground with her foot, as if oil might gush out of it. Harvey saw young girl's eyes in a face that was not much wrinkled.

'How long have you been doing this, then?' Ava asked.

'Twenty years. Since I packed in the pit.'

'Lorna told me about the accident.'

'Why have you come down to the yard? You could have phoned. I do *have* a phone.'

'I wanted to see you in your place of work. A man is at his most natural there, Ken used to say.'

'Did he now? How did he go, anyway?'

'Prostate cancer. Gets a lot of you, the doctor said. He was only sixty eight.'

Only two years older, Harvey thought, as he mumbled a condolence. It was so strange, the speed at which things could change, even in his life. It was unreal to be here with Ava in the yard, this decaying imprint of his life's drift. Ava surveyed the yard, hand on hip. Harvey caught her perfume in the slight breeze. It went well with the warm day.

'Much money in this?' Ava muttered.

Harvey shrugged and thought of the tins. He glowed with pride, secrecy, and a little shame.

'Used to be,' he answered, 'not so much now.'

'Still don't give anything away, do you?'

He shrugged again, but this time with a smile of apology.

'Things are changing in scrap. Cars are getting more complicated and I don't think scrappies have much of a future. In the old days—'

'I don't want to hear about the old days. Don't tell me that you've become one of those old fogies who look back all the time, have you? *Imagining* a better past, and bloody living in it.

'Come on,' Ava said. 'I'll take you for a drive, in something that actually goes.'

'I'll lock up, then.'

Harvey took off his overalls but knew he still smelt of oil. Ava drove out of the village, faster than Harvey was comfortable with.

'I bought this just before Ken died,' Ava said. 'I knew he didn't have long and I needed something to take me out of myself.'

They drove down the valley, to open spaces. Ava knew what she was about, and if driving had come late to her, at least it came naturally. She pulled into a pub on the edge of country.

'I've been here a few times before,' she said. 'I'll buy you a pint, since you aren't driving.'

They sat at a window table. Harvey excused himself immediately, the Gents a sanctuary where he could regain his composure. There was a smear of grease on his forehead, but Ava had not mentioned it, and his fingernails were ingrained with dirt. He couldn't believe she had brought him to a pub.

'You were gone a long time,' Ava said, 'weren't doing your hair, were you? I see you've still got most of it.'

They sat in silence for a while. Harvey was in no hurry to push the talk, because he didn't trust his tongue.

'You were never this quiet, as I remember,' Ava said. 'Full of it, you were.'

'I had it all before me then, and I knew nothing.'

'None of us did.'

Harvey felt her hand on his, warm and sure.

'The last thing Ken said was, don't stay on your own. Find someone else, he told me. There's plenty on their own, 'course I don't think he meant you, mind, but when Lorna mentioned you were still around I thought, why not?'

'Why not what?'

'Look you up, you silly sod. See how you were fixed.' Ava paused for a moment and Harvey felt the pressure on his hand increase. 'We never had children,' she murmured.

Harvey grew more comfortable with her hand, and put his other one on top of it.

'If Ken hadn't died we'd never have seen each other again. It's all going a bit fast,' he said.

'It has to, at our age. Anyway, you weren't so bad back then. Just too bloody full of yourself, always trying to be something you really weren't. Looking at you now I reckon time has cured that. Let's see what food they do here.'

Ava had settled it by the time she dropped him off at his house. They'd *see how it went* for a few months, and then she expected him to move down to the Vale with her. Sell up the yard and the house. Harvey told her a lot in a few hours. About the new road, and his financial comfort zone, which she could more than match. Alcohol and Ava unlocked his tongue, made it spin as it made up for years of reticence. He almost told her about the tins.

When they said goodbye Harvey felt like a kid inside and was still dazed when he saw the smoke pluming above the scrap yard, and heard the excited voices of children as they ran towards it.

Must be close to my place, Harvey thought. No, it *is* my place. He hurried down to the lane, overtaken by more sprightly neighbours.

'Looks like the whole lot is going up, Dick,' a young man yelled as he sped past.

The youngster was right. Harvey pushed through the crowd at the gates. No one went further. Inside, what could burn was burning. Several hundred wrecks were roasting, crashing down on each other, their insides aflame, petrol tanks going up with a whoosh, metal flying around like shrapnel. Sirens were getting louder, and then arriving. The crowd parted for the firemen but even they did not enter the yard. Not much point risking ourselves, the chief said. Not for old scrap. This man turned to Harvey.

'No one was working in there?' he asked.

'No, I'd closed for the day.'

'We'll just contain it from here, then.'

The estate car was well alight before Harvey remembered the next lot of money he'd been storing in the tin, and where he kept it. He lurched forward, tripping over one of the hoses that were being unfurled.

'Get back out of it, pop,' a fireman shouted, 'leave this to us.'

He was ushered back to the wide-eyed, entertained crowd.

It was a strange feeling. A lifetime's meanness was being challenged, just like it was challenged by Ava, and the emotions she brought to the table. A few days ago he would have been distraught, capable of running to his estate car safe, sifting crumbling hot ash with his scorched fingers and bellowing out his secret loss. A part of him still wanted to but it was a part rapidly diminishing, and he felt it fading away into the future he now saw.

Harvey started to laugh, quietly, lest they thought him shocked or mad. Each burning wreck was part of the joke. He turned away from the action and threaded his way back through the crowd, thinking of the first time he'd seen Ava in that swimsuit. It was dark red and she was just coming out of the sea, sun grasping at her glistening, salted, raven-black hair.

THE BOX ON THE MANTELPIECE

I watch as a muscular sea takes the small wooden box away from me. It bobs and ducks into the waves, drifting into the Baltic darkness, perhaps to be taken further and further north, until it is locked in ice. Perhaps I should have destroyed its contents, but I prefer to let nature deal with the unnatural. I want my hands to stay clean.

The box was always out of place in Manfred's austere apartment. It was a touch of decadent Vienna in the midst of austere Prussia. It was intricately worked mahogany, oblong and quite large, and made to hold a rich man's Cuban cigars, he said. Slender and fine-lined, it was the nearest thing to a feminine presence in my uncle's world.

Manfred wasn't very close to anyone, apart from me maybe, his sole nephew. He never liked close, he said he did not need it. Perhaps he didn't even understand it. For him the war had done for close. *I died with Der Führer,* he once said to me, when flush with Schnapps, in what was a curious voice for him. It was shot through with emotion, but I was not sure if it was full of love or hate. I was too young to really understand at the time, but his shocking words stayed with me. The war was a subject *verboten* in our household. Let the past lie where it belongs, father always said. Even then I knew that was the easy way out, the way my father always took.

Manfred did not smoke and I never knew what he kept in the box, if anything. It was opened with a silver key, which was attached to a thin chain he always kept on him, sometimes revealing it with a flourish as he pulled it from a waistcoat pocket. Revealing it, but never using it.

As a child I imagined all sorts of contents for this box. It became Pandora-like, and a minor joke between us. I'd ask what was in it, and get the usual cryptic replies in return, which was the nearest to *Kabaret* Manfred ever got.

As I grew older it became more of a chore to visit my uncle. I became mindful that my family thought him an embarrassment, someone who had turned his back on the new world, an ageing man who smelt permanently of soap, and dressed in clothes fashionable a generation ago. Manfred's tie was knotted so tightly around his neck it seemed to be slowly garrotting him, and his suits were dusty and drab. A dramatic under-achiever, the family judged, wasting his education, and his opportunities. Uncle Manfred was never one of us.

My visits stopped altogether when I went to college and met Eva. I forgot about the box, and what it might hold. I also forgot about uncle Manfred, more or less, until I received news of his demise.

The concierge found him, slumped in the corridor outside his apartment, with what she thought was his door key in his hand. Poor soul, she said, he was such a quiet, inoffensive man, a true gentleman.

Perhaps it was fate that I was in town at the time, trying

to drum up ever-diminishing business for my firm. The concierge phoned my mother with the news, using the address book Manfred kept by his phone, and I went round there, realising it had been more than ten years since I'd seen him.

Manfred had been laid out on his bed in anticipation of the undertaker, and seemed larger than I remembered him, or perhaps it was the narrow bed of a bachelor that made him seem so. Frau Kohl fussed around me, muttering, *poor man, poor man.* She pointed to the key on Manfred's chain. The concierge thought he must have been trying to get in when it happened, maybe about to phone for help. Doctor Franz says it was a heart attack, she told me, no doubt about it.

Uncle Manfred looked ready for his coffin. He was wearing one of his usual three-piece suits, a crisp white shirt and blue tie, but the tie was wrong. It was not a Manfred tie, for it had been loosened until it hung insecurely around his neck. He'd be mortified, I thought. His face still retained some of its florid glow, though a grey pallor had already begun to seep into it.

Frau Kohl was wrong about the key. It was the one for the box, not the door. I wondered why he had taken it from his pocket. It must have been his last action in this life. Did he need something in the box? Did he realise he was dying? I went into the living room. The box was in its usual place, everything in the apartment was how I remembered it, but more faded. Manfred lived in a sepia world, fixed in some point in his past. There was no television, just a scattering of books, and a few magazines on the kitchen table, men working out in various poses, an echo of my uncle's athletic youth, perhaps.

I managed to usher the concierge out. The doctor had made all the arrangements, and it would not be long before they came for my uncle. There would have to be a post mortem. Detaching the key from Manfred's waistcoat and feeling a little like I was robbing the dead, I went straight to the box. I felt compelled to do so. I brought it to the table and sat with it for a moment, hesitating, feeling I was violating his world, Manfred's sedate unchanging world, but one that I was beginning to think might hold many secret pathways.

I died with Der Führer. That strange, and shameful utterance from years ago came back to me. I saw again the look on Manfred's face as he said it, the hint of an enigmatic smile on his face, then the shrug of shoulders. I think it stayed in my mind because it was the one mention of the war from a family member in all my childhood. Six years had been wiped from our family history.

Manfred was a man who had drifted through life. He'd done nothing, achieved nothing. He just was. The stark bareness of his *Lebensraum* depressed me, but maybe guilt fuelled it, for my long selfish absence from a man always considerate and tolerant with me.

I turned the key in the lock and the box opened reluctantly. There were two compartments in it. In one was what seemed like ashes, and in the other an envelope. I took it out, opened it and recognised Manfred's hand. There were pages of his small, immaculate writing, almost copperplate in its perfection.

The urge to read it immediately was strong, but I

pocketed the letter, and left with the box secreted in my overcoat. It was theft, but I doubt that Manfred would have minded. It was fate that I was here, drawn to him in death and to the one object that bound our past together.

I walked out into a fine autumn morning to the park nearby, where I bought coffee and sat on a bench. Very young children passed by with their minders. They stared at me. Manfred had probably never been here, though it was just a few hundred metres from his door.

I put the box on the bench besides me and took the letter from my pocket. Manfred's fine hand sprang to life in my hands.

He never smokes or drinks, never has; that is the first thing that impresses me about him. He does not eat meat either. When I read this, I think how different he must be, amongst that crowd of self-servers and bourgeois hangers-on. He stands alone. When I pass close to him I know I am a head taller than he, but feel he is still looking down on me. I cease smoking, so I can be like him in this one thing, but drink is impossible to deny. How else could I survive these last days? It's a miracle worthy of the Führer himself that I do. Memories are vivid, they always will be for me, but they are soaked in alcohol. I drink whatever I can get and there is always plenty about in the bunker. The place is awash with it. The closer the shells the more most of us drink, from the generals to myself, the orderly-cum-valet. We all drift on an alcoholic sea, waiting for the wreck that is coming.

The sun bounced off the letter's white pages into me eyes. I shielded them as a young girl ran up to the bench to retrieve a ball. She smiled at me, her eyes innocent, but her minder came up quickly and guided the child away. Don't worry, I have two of my own, I wanted to say.

I wondered if I should read on, anxious about what I might find, and what implications there might be for the Kuhlmann family. I was sweating. It would be better to remove myself to a more private place. But I wanted to be out in the open, and for the box to be out in clean air. So I read on.

That I come to be here is another miracle. Me, Manfred Kuhlmann, a mere speck from the outer reaches of the Reich, picked up and placed at its heart. Attending to its very soul. My brother Otto would be amazed at where I've ended up. He has never understood my path in life. Otto worked hard in school and did well. I idled but did better, then lived a wastrel life thereafter whilst he chased success in business. It is understandable we have become distant. When my share of our father's money ran out it seemed natural that I ended up working in bathhouses, given the time I spent in them. It was repetitive, undemanding work, but I did not come home exhausted with the problems of trying to better myself. I could lock myself into who I was, what I was, and live the illicit, carnal life that nature always intended for me.

When the war comes I continue with this work in the army, after the obligatory training of a soldier, which the Wermacht and I agree is hopeless in my case. I was lucky with my sergeants, they defer to my class, rather than bear down on it, so I got through it, and am transferred to laundry duties and the like. By the time France falls I am in Berlin, working for a major, an aide to one of the chiefs of staff. We are friendly, and he treats me more as an equal than valet.

I have brief glimpses of the Führer in these early days. The wonderful days when his will cascades over Europe. He is vibrant, bursting with energy and self-belie,f and I feel his fervour, share it as it surges through my sluggish veins, giving me an enthusiasm I have never felt for anyone or anything before. A gap in my life is being filled and I love him for it.

The chance comes to go to Berchtesgaden. I can't believe it. The major is transferred there, much to my delight, if not his. Major Gruber is a secretive man, a career officer, and I'm not sure where his affiliations lie, but I can hardly contain myself. I am to be part of a small, hand-picked staff. For the first time in my life I am needed.

My first glimpse of Berchtesgaden transfixes me. Eagle's Eyrie is the perfect name for it. It's a magnificent setting, commanding a perfect sweep of the surrounding mountains, a location that inspires me, and emphasises our leader's grandeur. It makes me think of my roots, and be proud of them. All those parental words I grew up with, and ignored, now take on meaning. Fate is controlling my life, it's stopped me drifting and given me something to belong to – Manfred Kuhlmann, valet in charge of the linen. His linen. And they make me a corporal, as he had been in the last war.

There was a gap in the writing and a smear of grease on the bottom of the page, which is very un-Manfred like. I imagined him writing in various locations, perhaps always carrying the pages on him. I was alone in the park now, and it was getting colder, wind sifting brown leaves about my feet. It was hard to believe what I was reading, but I turned to the next page to find Manfred has moved forward several years, to the end of the war. There is a change in his mood.

As Berchtesgaden was Eden so the Chancellery becomes hell, and the bunker is its gateway. The old place is just a dream now, as the ground all around shakes with the nearing conflict, muffled sounds that never stop. My mood darkens as hope fades.

The week Roosevelt dies I hear Goebbels say to the Führer that things might improve now. No, it's too late, he says, the whole world is against me. I am attending to something in the corner of the room, and I catch his eye. It is as if he is looking into my soul, that he knows my most intimate thoughts, and is thanking me for being part of his dream. To be here is the ultimate honour, and I will hold onto this until the end.

When the air raids become severe we move from the Chancellery to the bunker that has been prepared in its grounds. I am one of the few trusted to be here and have formed a close friendship with Heinz, the Führer's personal valet. With him, I try to ensure our leader's comfort and maintain standards of cleanliness, which is difficult, such is the enclosed nature of this place. I also have to deal with Frau Braun, which is difficult. Various chiefs come and go but she is always here. I don't understand the relationship and concentrate on our leader, and take heart from his.

Today is the Führer's birthday. Our enemies mark it with a ferocious air raid. The sky is incandescent with hellish colour; assorted reds bleed into black and orange, and what searchlights we have left try to cut through this. And all the time, just hundreds of metres away from us now, comes the sound of the Bolsheviks' advance, bludgeoning their way into our city, fighting against German boys and old men. Buildings shake constantly with the crump of mortars, and heavier guns, a continual thunder that never calms. The beast from the east is coming.

I was close to the end of Manfred's writings now. Blue sky had been pushed out, as clouds congealed into a leaden covering of the sky. It was even threatening to snow, but I was still hot. My shirt stuck to my back and my cheeks burned, as if I was with Manfred at the heart of that Berlin inferno. My uncle had made Hitler a deity, and I was burning with shame for his grotesque judgement, and for my family's sly concealing of Manfred's past. Maybe Manfred was a symbol of the collective madness of those times, and the evil done. I thought about stuffing the pages into a bin, washing my hands of them and getting away, but I had to finish reading them. I felt it was my duty.

Today Bormann orders luggage to be packed for Berchtesgaden, but we'll never leave here now. He orders us all to go but Braun refuses to leave, and the rest of us take her lead. A telegram comes from Goering. He claims leadership of the Reich. So, the rats are rising up from the ship. Heinz pours us two large glasses of Schnapps and we drink quietly together. This really is the end, he says. It is April 22, a time when nature should be renewing itself, casting off the gloom of winter. It is a most terrible few hours, but despite the chaos around me I manage to drift into sleep.

I am awakened by a shot. Then another. For weeks such noises have been a constant backdrop, but these come from inside the bunker. Heinz is shaking me, he's greatly agitated, his large frame wracked, as if he's sobbing inside, and trying to suppress it. Powerful people are running around the bunker, ignoring us. Heinz leads me to Hitler's private room. He is on a sofa, leaning to one side, a trickle of blood leaking from his temple. Eva is with him, her legs drawn up, her lips clamped together, as if concentrating deeply on something.

Dead, Heinz gasps, they are both dead. For a long moment I am frozen, my eyes locked on our leader's face, willing it back to life. Shock prevents any movement, but Heinz has greater presence of mind. Come, we have our orders, he says. He lifts up the Führer easily, and I carry Braun. Her head falls back and I can't look at her. We crouch and stagger up to the bunker entrance and out into the Chancellery grounds. Truly we are in the underworld, for all hell is here. The air is acrid with smoke, and we keep as low to the ground as possible. All my senses are acute, I feel I'm inside every explosion, that every bullet is coming for me, but I keep my eyes down.

I'm not sure how many people are with us: Bormann perhaps, and others. Someone lays a small rug on the ground, and the bodies are placed on it. Heinz has procured cans of gasoline from somewhere, and he pours them over the bodies and quickly sets them alight. We watch the pyre, oblivious of anything else. The rest go back inside but I stay with Heinz until the flames have done their work. With that amount of gasoline it does not take long. Heinz hands me a jar. Here, he says, I can't do it. We must keep something. He pushes me forward and I use the jar as a scoop to collect the ashes.

Minutes later, we are following Bormann through the sewers. He seems to know the way to the underground, but I see nothing, feel nothing. My legs move, pushed on by Heinz, but I'm not part of this motion. I am still back there, in the bunker, with that last vision. Bormann leaves us suddenly, vanishing into the crowd that is milling around at the main station.

Heinz is shouting. He's telling me to get a hold of myself. Go home, he says, back to your people. You are lucky you live in the west. Come with me, I hear myself say, but he refuses, and after embracing me, he too is gone. I am alone, one of a despairing crowd, blind with panic, all desperate to escape the Russians. I have a small case Heinz packed for me and the jar is inside, nestled amongst dirty underclothes. I follow others along the tracks, often stumbling but *never relaxing my grip on the case. We are ascending steps and are out into the city again, but farther away from the guns. I'm walking west, homewards. On the outskirts of the city I turn for a final look and my heart is broken like the buildings, the remnants of which litter the bloody skyline like huge shattered teeth.*

I thought I had come to the end but there was more on the back of the last sheet of paper.

May 1. 1950. A fine May Day, when the weather would encourage hope in most people. I am settled in this apartment now, and I will not leave it. Last week I bought a handsome cigar box, an Austrian antique that cost me a week's pay. I give the box pride of place on my mantelpiece. This will the last resting place for the Führer. No one will ever know, now whilst I live. Theories abound about his last days – well, let them. I will leave these writings in the box with him, and one day they will become someone else's responsibility. What a stir they would cause, but his secret is mine.

The years after the war have been hard, and there is less and less contact with the family. They want to be part of the new half-Germany, and of course they are right. They must move on. I cannot.

A week later I sat amongst a small group at Manfred's funeral, recognising some, not knowing others. The Kuhlmann family has been scattered, first by the war, then by a disinterested distance. I loathed funerals, the ritual, the uneasy mix of true mourners, false ones, and the mildly curious who don't really belong. Manfred wouldn't have approved, why bother, would have been his comment. The phrase could serve as his motto, certainly for the post-war Manfred I knew, or thought I knew. Now I wondered what had gone on in his head. I felt that much was left unsaid in the writings I found. I didn't want to think what Manfred might have taken part in, because it made me sick to my stomach.

An old man stifled tears in the row in front of me. He made no noise but I saw his large body trembling, and the handkerchief pressed to his mouth. He turned and looked at me, his wrinkled face moist under the eyes, which were the palest blue, and seemed too young for his face. I knew this must be Heinz. He too had survived. I acknowledged him with a nod, but said nothing. When Manfred's coffin slid down I got away quickly.

I did not take long to make a decision about the box. Watery oblivion would be a fitting end for the ashes from that vile time. Before going home I make a detour north, to the sea.

WORKING ON THE RAILWAY

'It went wrong from the start. The way we gave in, it was unbelievable. I'd only been out for a few weeks. My guts were just starting to get used to the place. Then I was holding my arms up to little men on bikes, men we outnumbered five to one. Our sergeant, Davies, had been in the first war, and he kept saying that nothing ever changes. We'll always be led by donkeys.

Jack stopped, snorting away a dewdrop as he rubbed at his eyes. 'Lions led by donkeys,' he muttered. His eyes were usually moist these days, blue smudges sunk well back in a face of worn cracks. His birthday cards were on his lap and his 80 badge hung loosely from his cardigan.

Jack wiped a hand across his face and dug into his tobacco pouch, allowing most of the weed to fall through his shaky fingers onto the newspaper on his lap. He used this to funnel loose bits and pieces back into his pouch. Jack managed to make a bent roll-up which his friend Ron lit for him.

'Still got a steady hand, I see,' Jack said. 'Steadier then mine, anyway.'

Jack drew heavily on his smoke, and settled back into his armchair, rocking it slightly. His eyes closed.

'Is he on about the war again?' Jennie said, as she entered

the room. 'Sometimes I feel like *I* was a prisoner of the Japanese.'

Jennie emptied Jack's ashtray, then sat next to him, taking the cigarette away from her father before it burnt his fingers.

'I'm surprised he even got three cards,' Ron whispered. 'I never thought Jack would last this long, and here we are entering the new millennium.'

'He'll never leave this one,' Jennie said.

'Aye. Jack's not one for change, or letting things go.'

Jennie put her father's cards on the mantelpiece, moving the picture of her mother to one side. She wondered if it would have been different if she could have given her parents grandchildren. Jack might have softened a little. Ron was right; it was amazing her father has lasted so long, considering the condition he'd been in when he returned from the war. He'd outlived his wife by almost twenty years and Jennie's own man by ten. It was also her birthday in a few days. Fifty, it didn't bear thinking about.

'I'll pop off then,' Ron said.

Ron got up with difficulty, resting a hand on Jack's shoulder for a moment. As he left, pushing himself along the road with his stick, Ron's thoughts raced back more than sixty years, to that heady summer of '39. He could almost taste the warm beer, smell the stale but comforting air of Player's fags, and hear the excited voices of his mates as they voiced their enthusiasm to do the right thing. Jack's birthday brought it all back, his lifelong mate had a way of cutting through time like it wasn't there.

Jennie went into the kitchen to tidy up. It was large and

old, in a house that was also large and old, too large and too old, for just the two of them. It was her childhood home and she'd drifted back into it. The house was a place of the past, her father's past. He was a man soaked in strikes, loss and the Japanese, a bitter trinity bound together with stubborn pride

The newspaper cutting Jennie had thought about all week lay on the kitchen table. Her friend Ann had given it to her.

'You're not too old for this,' Ann said, 'I've checked. People our age are reliable, and you can work hours that suit, flexitime, they call it. You could do the twilight shift. Old Jack only sits in his chair in the evening, messing around with his books.'

'He still goes down the Cross Inn.'

'Only once a week now, and it's called The Golden Age now, Jen.'

'Why?'

'Search me. They like to change things now, I suppose. If you got out more you'd see that a lot is changing around here. Look, phone up Human Resources. I've already put in a word.'

'Human what?

'Personnel. They've changed that name too. Look, it will be good for you to get you out again, and the money will be useful. You've been rotting away in here since Ed died.' Ann softened her voice as Jennie flinched a little. 'Jack likes you here being a replacement wife and mother to him, putting food on the table whenever he wants it, doing everything for him. But what happens when he goes? It might be years yet, and you'll be stuck on your own. You're hardly ancient and you've still got a bit of a figure, you lucky bugger. There's plenty of men around, not all of them useless either.'

Jennie stared at her friend.

'Well, not totally useless. Maybe you can find a toyboy to take you away from this mausoleum.'

'Don't be so ridiculous.'

'Christ, I never liked this house when we were kids. Too many shadows.'

Ann's words came back to Jennie as she put away the tea things. *Too many shadows, too many memories.* She imagined her father's reaction if she took the job.

When the Japanese had first appeared in the valley he'd been livid, but the '74 strike had kept her father busy at the time. It had been his one moment of real triumph when that strike was won and the government fell. She'd been more interested in getting to know Edward at the time, but at least the house had been lighter for a while. Lighter in spirit.

Jennie made her decision the next morning. She saw to Jack's breakfast, treated his birthday hangover, and then phoned the number Ann had given her. She was offered an interview the next day. It was as quick and as easy as that.

'Who are you phoning?' Jack shouted from the kitchen.

'Ann,' she answered.

The next day Jennie told her father she was going down the shops. She knew he wouldn't notice that she was dressed up. Jack was reading at the kitchen table, his battered glasses on the end of his nose, crumbs scattered over the pages of one of his history books. Jennie stood behind his chair.

'Why don't you go for a walk,' she said. 'It's a lovely day.'

'Been walking all my life,' Jack muttered.

'I didn't think you'd do it,' Ann said, 'not really,' when Jennie phoned her.

'I haven't got the job yet.'

'You'll get it. I've been singing your praises to Mr. Matsuoko for weeks now, and I'm a section leader, don't forget.'

Matsuoko. The man's name made Jennie shudder a little. She wondered if she could ask Ron to tell her father. No, too cowardly, even for her.

Jack was restless. For him, time was getting harder to spend. The girl was right, the sky was blue outside. He *would* go for a walk and unlike Ron, he did not need a stick.

As he walked, the sun warmed his back, and at least the air pretended to be fresh. He reached the park at the end of the street where a mother, Jack thought a child herself, pushed her four years old girl on a swing.

A light breeze fought against the sunshine. How Jack had longed for any sort of breeze on that railway. All they got was fetid air churned up by thousands of over-heated bodies, each one smelling like hell. Since Mary had died he could not stop his thoughts going back there. Images re-awakened, as clear as this spring morning, and Jack began to sweat. For him, that damned railway had never stopped being built, it was an endless track through his mind. Maybe this was *his* price for victory. They'd all had to pay one, winners and losers.

'Hello, Mr Evans,' the little girl said, prompted by her mother.

'Hello, princess.'

Jack walked on but thought better of the Cross Inn, or whatever it was called now. He might become too maudlin there, like those old boys of the First War he used to avoid as a young man. He understood them better now, much better.

Jack made his way home along the lane at the top of the village. Everything on the valley floor was changed, but the lane was much the same as it had ever been. The trees were older, more gnarled, some twisted into strange shapes by subsidence. Many were close to their end, but they kept their station all the same, reliable sentinels that they were. This place was too high up for change, too far away from the action.

Looking down, Jack saw the new factories laid out in uniform slabs of concrete and steel. The Japanese one was the largest. It was near the shaft of the old pit, the first one to close, and it flew the Union Jack alongside a company flag that was not unlike the Rising Sun. Jack did not care for either flag. He remembered the hoo-hah when they first arrived in the valley. The tub-thumping, the new-beginnings speeches, and those false dawns his country seemed to specialise in. He knew better. People only ever came to Wales to take out. Always had and always will, he mouthed to himself.

Ann was right, Jennie thought. The questions were easy, almost perfunctory. Was she good with her hands? Yes. Could she work shifts? Yes. Did she have young children? No. She was flattered by this question. When could she start? Any time.

They made it the next Monday, on a six-month rolling contract. Jennie felt exhilarated as she walked home. A cage door was being opened, but now she had to get past the ringmaster.

Jack was irritated. Where was the girl? It was Friday, they always had fish on Friday, but the house was free of cooking, and free of his daughter. Jack sat in his armchair and thumbed through the morning paper, but soon threw it down. It was all so-called celebrities and disasters. He heard the front door opening.

'You on strike or what?' Jack asked, as soon as Jennie came in.

'Oh, you're back, dad.'

'Of course I'm back – it's dinnertime.'

'I had to go out.'

'I don't see any shopping.'

'I had to see about something.'

'You know I like a bit of fish on a Friday, not—'

'I went to see about a job,' Jennie interrupted.

'That the cod is much use these days. No taste in it at all.'

'Dad, did you hear what I said.'

'What?'

'A job. I said I've been for an interview.'

'What the hell are you talking about?'

'Ann sorted it out for me.'

'You haven't got time to do a bloody job. Hang on, Ann works for that TV lot. You're not telling me you're thinking of working for the Japs?'

'Not thinking about it. They've offered me a job and I've taken it. I start Monday.'

Jennie was breathing hard as Jack got up from his chair and came towards her. For a moment she thought he might strike her. She looked into his watery eyes and saw the small blue scars on his face stand out as it reddened. Jack just stood there, lost for words. It had taken Jennie half a century to impress her father. She forced an apology away from her lips.

Jack sat down again, confused, and still silent. He seemed smaller, his shoulders sagging as he dug fiercely into his tobacco pouch. Bits spilled out onto his trousers. Finally, as his smoke was made, Jack found his voice.

'You never said a word,' he muttered, 'not a bloody word. We've always managed, with my pension and your Ed's insurance money.'

'It's not a question of managing, dad.'

'They don't own the valley, you know. There's other jobs, if you're so keen to get out of here.'

'Maybe, but this is the one on offer, and Ann's already there.'

'Ann! That girl never did have any sense, the only thing she can do is spend money like it's going out of fashion. That's what this comes down to, isn't it? Cash. That's why that lot are here in the first place – taking advantage of our so-called flexible work force.'

'You're going to make yourself ill again,' Jennie said quietly.

'I'll get your dinner on,' she said, leaving the room abruptly.

Jack's eyes moistened with rage and frustration. Jennie's

bosses down at that factory might be the sons of his tormentors.

He smoked his roll-up. It seared his chest as he sucked hard, making his worn out lungs suffer. He'd always smoked this way. Fags had been currency in Burma, a man could barter with them. Survive. Harsh voices began to bark in his head, blistered hands grabbed inadequate tools, insects ate him alive, and the sun ripped his back.

Jennie prepared the food automatically. She understood the way her father was, for her mother had always slaved over him, and Jack had lost her early. Jack ate his dinner in silence. Jennie showed no sign of changing her mind, or even apologising. Afterwards he phoned Ron to meet him in the pub that afternoon.

'Where's the fire?' Ron asked.

'What?'

'Well it must be some kind of emergency, for us to be here at this time.'

Jack tried to keep calm as he told his tale but the words still came out in sharp bursts.

'She hasn't even said sorry,' Jack said, as an afterthought.

Ron sipped his pint quietly.

'Well, what do you think, Ron?'

'Learn to cook, I'd say.'

'Is that supposed to be funny?'

'Sorry. Look, Jack.'

'What?'

'I see your point, of course I do, but that war was half a bloody century ago. I let it go years ago, and it's about time you did. Don't cash in your chips being haunted by the past. Yes, it still gets in my head sometimes, but I didn't want the rest of my life dominated by drowning sailors covered in oil, blokes on fire in engine rooms. I'd be fighting that damn war for the rest of my life. Like you are.'

'You think the girl's right, then?'

'She's just trying to move on. Shame her and Ed didn't have kids. They might have mellowed you a little.'

Jack snorted into his beer. He thought of Ron's bustling household, awash with grandchildren, noise and colour. Then he thought of his own bare place.

'But working for those bastards though,' Jack said, his voice dwindling.

'But they're not *those bastards* any more, just foreigners working here.'

'The house is quiet enough as it is.'

'Don't tell me you are complaining about that. You can borrow some of my brood if you want.'

Jack grunted and they were quiet for a while. Ron looked at his friend of seventy years, and regretted his words. Jack looked so tired, and overwhelmed.

'Lost in your thoughts, Jack?'

'Got a lot of them to get lost in.'

'As have we all. Yours tend to run riot, though. Want another?'

'No. Best be getting back.'

'Look, do you want me to come with you?'

'What, for moral support or to keep the peace?'

'Whatever.'

'No, you're all right. Thanks though, Ron.'

The house *was* empty. It had never felt emptier. They had bought it in the late fifties with the money Mary had been left, and his rising miners' wages. Mary had planned to fill it with kids but that had not happened. Just Jennie.

There was a note on his armchair. *Dad, be back by six. Will do you tea then.* He screwed it up and flicked it into the fire grate. They still had a real fire, a museum piece that had become fashionable again. Jack sat in front of it and closed his eyes. He saw his daughter when she came back from the hospital that last time. It had been raining and he first thought it was that which had soaked her face.

Jack roused himself, got up, and went into the kitchen, with Ron's words fresh in his head. He opened the fridge cautiously. There was plenty of the salad stuff that Jennie was always trying to feed him. He started to prepare food. Jack took time to find things, and was glad that there was some cooked ham. Proper ham, not that wrapped up shiny stuff. He tried to remember how Mary had done this.

It took him some time to be satisfied with his work, arranging and re-arranging the food on the table several times before he went back into the living room. There he began to shake a little. It was useless trying to make a smoke.

When Jennie came in she went straight to the kitchen. Jack thought he heard her gasp.

'Dad, what's going on?' Jennie was standing in the living room doorway. 'You've done the tea.'

'Yes.'

There was shock on Jennie's face. 'It's the way mam used to do ham and salad,' she said.

'Is it?'

Jack got up and followed Jennie into the kitchen. She sat down awkwardly and stared at the ham arranged in a circle.

'Do you want some of that wine we had for my birthday?' Jack asked. 'There's still half a bottle.'

'Dad, are you trying to get me to change my mind?'

'No. I know I couldn't.'

'What then?'

Jack pushed some of the ham around on his plate.

'Perhaps I'm telling you I *can* do things for myself, if I have to. I was in the army, or didn't you know that?'

Jennie sipped her wine, wondering if her father had attempted a joke.

'It's only part time,' she said, 'afternoons and early evening.'

'Aye, I know. The twilight shift.'

Jack had never liked wine much. It was slippery customer that crept up on you. He swirled his around in the glass, and saw many faces swirl with it. He could only name a few now, the ones who had died quickly, or had lasted until the end.

'See how you get on,' Jack said. 'You might want to go full time later.'

TREMLETT'S TIME

Tremlett's cycle wobbles as he pedals to work, its age conspiring with his own and the pot-holed roads. He passes the small park, as he has done for forty years, its trees flush with autumn, and turning gold as the sun gets up. The ornamental pond flashes him a silver salute. At this early in the morning the park is empty and its gates still locked. It seems bigger without people, like a piece of real country.

Tremlett stops to buy a paper and the ten cigarettes he always smokes in work. They divide his day into ten neat sections. He's glad they're selling packets of ten again, a recession is always good for something.

He cycles through the foundry gates with some trepidation, for this is his last day. His gold watch day. There will be drinking over the road afterwards, and he'll be the centre of attraction, for a few minutes. Tremlett the Castings, forty years before the fires. The nickname has stuck from the old days, despite the fact that he is now a sweeper-up of swarf, endlessly pushing his eighteen-inch brush around the foundry floor.

Tremlett pushes his brush until mid-morning. The foundry is slack, finishing up bits and pieces and dreaming of the big orders that no longer come. A chill day blows itself in through open doors to contest the air with the fires, so

Tremlett stays as close to the heat as he can. Near the girls from Delhi. Unlike the young lads these are polite to him, and he likes their musical chat, even if he can't understand it, and he likes the fact they are here, usurping the old order. It should go against the grain, these girls taking the work of local men, but it doesn't bother him, they too are locals, now. The foundry has become a crazy place; with the new regime, nastiness and double-dealing are the norm now. Tremlett is glad to be finishing.

A hand is placed on Tremlett's shoulder. It's Morgan, the foreman.

'Mr. Allinson wants to give a bit of a speech after dinner, Trem. You'll have your watch then. Dare say the morning boys will take you over the Inn after. It's tradition.'

The watch, it is a last link with the past. Everything else has gone. As new blood filters through the gates Tremlett notices how thin it is, how low its expectations. Unions squashed, men cowed until they are no longer men, cowed until it becomes a permanent state of mind, a way of being, a way of surviving. He's a survivor himself.

Tremlett pushes the swarf past the Indian girls. One gives him a toffee. It sticks to his top set and concentrates his thoughts, which are miles away, in the land of his hopeful youth. He realises Morgan is talking to him.

'Come on, Trem, you dozy old bugger, get washed up. Mr. Allinson wants to give you the watch in the canteen.'

The speech is the usual verbal bumph, and this new man Allinson even coughs in the usual places. For a sweeper Tremlett doesn't come out too badly. He's eulogised into a loyal and trusted worker, who *has been with us for a very long time.* This makes him grimace and lock his face into what he thinks is a gesture of gratitude, knowing that he's being watched by a hundred pairs of eyes. By mouthing his easy platitudes, Allinson can pretend that things haven't changed, and that he, Tremlett, represents the timelessness of the foundry, but the only thing that haven't changed are the platitudes.

Tremlett feels that perhaps he should worry more about the way his work place has changed, that he at least owes the young this, but he's tired of it all, of the bullshit and empty words. None of it means as much as an hour on his clarinet which he has played tolerably well since his national service days. The early jazz of Goodman, Ellington, even Beiderbecke, old stuff, but good stuff. He has increased his playing since Edna died, and with the boy in New Zealand now he has lots of time to fill. Music provides some comfort, and the clarinet was always a good friend. Now it's his salvation as well.

Allinson hands him a wristwatch in an open box. It has a gold-plated top. Tremlett has never worn one. He comes out of his thoughts and accepts the watch, mumbling thanks with the handshake. There's a ripple of applause that doesn't get any louder, then the rush to the canteen counter. Management fades from the scene. For a moment Tremlett is left standing on his own. There's tightness in his chest as if a hand fingers his heart, and his arm tingles. He knows it's just nerves and takes a place at the end of a long table.

'No more brush pushing, Trem,' a young man says.

'Coming over the pub, Trem?' another asks.

'Whadya mean, is he coming over?' a third voice adds. 'He got no choice.'

This is true. Tremlett knows he'll have to mix, this once. Eating his cottage pie, he thinks the pub a final price to pay. He goes to his locker to clear out his things, then back into the foundry to say goodbye to the girls. They giggle from behind hands and for a moment he's back out there, haggling in the markets, buying a scarf for the girl he would marry back in Blighty.

Edna never understood the clarinet. When she was alive it was all covert practice, when she was out shopping, or secreted away in the shed. If the dog didn't start barking he was usually all right.

Theirs had been a prickly relationship from the start. His easiness, which Edna called lack of ambition, against her drive. Countless times he'd pushed the bike into a cutting east wind with the echoes of her disappointment in his ears. And she blamed him for the boy going. Bernard is a teacher now, at a school that has countryside for a back yard. Tremlett thought Bernard followed his mother, in setting himself a goal and achieving it, but she'd missed their son too much to ever agree. Tremlett missed *her*, despite their fractious history, and felt cheated she would not share his retirement. Perhaps she might have mellowed, not having to see him in demeaning overalls. He sighs. Of course she wouldn't have mellowed, but he still missed her.

'Trem, 'gis a look at that watch, worth a bit, that is.'

Within minutes they are taking him over the road, pushing him on as if he was a trophy, or victim. They surge along the bank of the flat grey slug of a river, then over the triple arched stone bridge to their place of worship. The legendary *Inn*.

'Stop worrying about your bloody bike, Trem. One of the boys will stick it in his van later. You and all.'

Tremlett is with some of the most dedicated drinkers of the foundry, boys who can down a pint in one as they seek to cool the heat of their workplace. He's not sure of the names of one or two, but knows each raw face, and how they stumble into work at six in the morning, their faces red and puffed, hair sticking up like matchsticks, guts rumbling. To tell their tales of women and fights, as they sweat out their night on their long shift. It amazes him how old some of them look, at thirty.

The group settles into the back lounge. Retirement binges always take place in the lounge. Tradition again. Ale flows freely, and some order two pints each, the first to slake their fiery thirst, the second to be drunk at a more leisurely pace. Perhaps foundries and breweries have always worked in tandem like this.

Tremlett's first pint of dark hits home quickly. He'd forgotten how potent the stuff was. He swills the liquid around a little, and wonders how much rubbish is concealed in its gloom, but sups it up with an outward show of enthusiasm. One of the men, Howley, takes it on himself to 'look after' Tremlett, which means plying him with drink, patronising his age and assuming control over the group.

'Trouble with you lot,' Howley says, 'you don' know what work is. Old Trem here grew up the 'ard way, din' you, butt? Not like this bunch of ponces.'

Howley has got it all wrong, Tremlett thought. His *time*

had been one of real apprenticeships, lasting employment and regular hours. The money in foundry work was always poor but there had been satisfaction in the job, and a fair degree of security. He thinks of telling them this but keeps his own counsel. Just as soon tell them what it's like on the moon, he thought, the dark side. How can he explain it, when the few men who read tabloid newspapers in work are now looked on as brainy.

An impromptu darts match begins, and Howley splits the gathering into two teams. Some have already drunk enough to miss the board. Tremlett throws his three arrows and is applauded. How he longs to be released, but there is no avoiding the beer and he knows he's slipping into the same state as the rest, but much quicker.

Images from his past begin to parade through his dazed mind. Years flick over like pages in his head, bustling, orderly, disorderly memories. There's Edna, in her bright seaside frock that looked like an advert for fruit salad, and the boy running over the sand and whizzing with energy. With his shock of blond curls Tommy looked like a young angel then. Then Tremlett sees Tommy the young man leaving for New Zealand, shepherded away to that far-off place by his English girlfriend, *stolen* away, Edna says. He hears her temper reverberating down all the years, she used it to counter her broken heart. Tremlett used his clarinet to counter his, in the summer warmth of the shed. His refuge.

When the girlfriend became wife and grandchildren came it didn't help. They were far-away faces never actually met. *How could we possibly afford to go there,* Edna used to say, or wail, if she'd had a few Emva Creams.

186

'Come on, Trem, it's your go, again,' Howley shouts. 'Go for double top. Jesus Christ, stop swaying, mun. Eh lads, the old boy's well on his way here. Get him another pint, someone.'

Tremlett *is* unsteady, but manages to avoid peppering the lurid wallpaper with his dart. Its deep red is getting in his eyes. He tries to blink it out but it will not go. There's now a full-blown party going on. Girls from the factory next to the foundry have joined them and their presence means that he is forgotten, and Tremlett thanks God for that.

Tremlett sits down, pushing his pint away as he watches couples pair off. Men slobber boozy invites, the drink making them think that they are other people, leading other lives. He hears a girl shout, *what's it all in aid of, then?* Someone points Tremlett out but the girl only spares him a second's glance. Music begins to pump from speakers on the walls, as loud as the times. He doesn't know what it is, and doesn't understand it. He hears noise but no crafted sound. It's definitely not the old stuff.

Tremlett's bemused eyes focus on Howley's hand trying to run its way up a girl's black jeans. Her colourful rebuff rings in his ears and lager is thrown over the laughing Howley.

There is pain. Knives run up his arm and begin to carve their way into his chest. There's a crushing there, as if a rock was resting on him. Tremlett attempts to fight it off, and thinks of shouting out, but it seems pointless. He tries to see the time on his new watch but its face is blurred. It seems to him that time his frozen. The pub goes quiet, and very dark.

'Oi,' Howley says, 'don' go to sleep, Trem. You've only 'ad two pints. Christ, it's your do, after all.'

He shakes Tremlett by the shoulders, quite roughly, and is joined by others.

THE BOOK OF COWLIN

'Oi, Cowlin,' a voice shouted out of the night, 'whadya writing then?'

The voice threw a piece of pasty at Cowlin's window. It was a good shot. Corned beef entrails flattened against the glass and slowly dribbled down. Youths grouped in the street below Cowlin's window, slouched against each other in ragged disorder, each an inebriate link in an invisible chain. They had seen Cowlin's desk lamp on, and his face trapped within its pool of light.

Cowlin expertly rolled a thin cigarette in a show of complete disdain, lit it in cupped hands and took a long drag. The boys lurched away, splitting up as they found their own houses, their derision fading into the night. Cowlin saw one totter and tumble into a puddle of his own making as he tried to piss against a wall. It made him smile.

Early next morning Cowlin was back at his workstation, his fox-red thinning hair and heavily-lined face making him look much older than the thirty-eight he was. His was a large frame and his hod carriers' hands punched the keys too hard. He smoked his first of the day, and watched sheep eat their way down the hillside in a straggly grey line. They stood out well against a slagheap that was scornful of any attempts to landscape it. Cowlin wondered if the sheep knew they were now considered clichés.

Ma Enoch sauntered past his window. Ma looked like Les Dawson trying to impersonate a woman. She had the same habit of heaving up her sizeable bosom and gumming vacantly as she stared nosily around her. The old woman glanced up at his window and was puzzled by the piece of dried pasty that had resolutely kept in place through the night. She scowled, at Cowlin and his world. She thought of books in the same light as something she stepped on, and people who wrote them somewhat lower.

Ma's old man, Emrys, had been Cowlin's first contact on the estate. Em was part of the furniture of the 'Spite pub, one of a table of Welsh caricatures that held court in the lounge corner. In those days, before his books had become common knowledge, Em had talked to him and shared a few stories.

Seeing Ma's broad backside manoeuvre itself through the shop's door Cowlin thought back to the first time he'd met her husband. Emrys had approached him at the bar on his first visit there.

'Not from around here, are you?' the old man asked.

Cowlin agreed he was not.

'What you doing on the estate then? Christ, no one comes here out of choice, do they? Desperate, like, are you?'

No, but he was broke.

'Somewhere to live,' Cowlin answered.

Emrys eyed him suspiciously before he rejoined his cronies. Yes, Cowlin was an outsider, an uneasy state here that muddled between good fortune and cardinal sin. If his trade was added, he became hopelessly alien.

Despite this gruff first meeting Emrys became an occasional visitor to Cowlin's flat. He had a scattering of books, bashed paperbacks and ex-library stock, which he thought gave him the fuel to drive his paper-thin knowledge, and link himself with Cowlin.

The one-eyed whimsy of Emrys passed for wisdom in this kingdom of the blind. He was of the generation that had flocked to the new kitchens and bathrooms of council houses.

'It was alright,' Em said, 'after the war. They had rules a mile long for this place, but it was all new. Indoor bogs, hot water, big gardens, they were all wonderful novelties in those days. Christ, there was even a stove in the kitchen, a gas stove. And we kept this place in good nick for years, right up 'til the sixties. Then it began to change. Families started to break up; girls brought up kids on their own, things started to fall apart. Anyone with a bit of sense got out. Oh aye, we had plenty blokes like you here then, them that went to the County School, but you couldn't see their dust. Some went back to the terraces, which had changed by then, mind. They had extensions and new doings, and people started to paint them in bright colours.'

Emrys became a useful source. Cowlin was able to take fragments of what the old man said and work it into his fiction, but the last thing he gleaned from Em was a real gem. Ma stopped him coming around after that.

It was a sodden day in April, solid rain sheeting down, hillsides obscured by low cloud. Everything painted a uniform grey. Emrys stopped in on his way back from his afternoon at the 'Spite.

'Jesus, it's cats and dogs out there,' he muttered, as he showered the room with liquid. 'Get us a cup of tea, kid.'

'Been with the lads?' Cowlin asked, visualising the row of crumbling, geriatric faces.

'Don' I always? Aye, they're a good bunch.'

Cowlin controlled a smile and fed his guest tea and encouragement. In return he received the story of Evans and Enid.

Emrys went into his story-telling mode, stretching back expansively and clicking his empty pipe against his new teeth. He still had most of his hair, silver tufts now but still with a memory of black in them, and neat white side-burns curled towards his mouth like a clown's smile. He had watery blue eyes that matched his mining scars.

'The funny thing is,' Emrys began, 'is that Evans seemed quite normal early on, chased skirt like the rest of us. That's how he took up with Enid Osborne, lucky bugger. But being with her must have turned him, somehow.'

'How do you mean, and who's this Enid woman anyway?'

'Who was she, you mean. She snuffed it, about ten years ago. Enid's life was hard, very hard. I can still remember her at school; pretty little thing, she was. That's what started her trouble, I 'spose. She got pregnant, back in thirty-four. She was only fourteen and never said who the father was. Her lot were a waste of space and wouldn't help her at all, and it was serious stuff in them days. There was only one thing to do, as far as the bastard authorities were concerned.'

'What?'

'They locked her up, didn't they? In a loony bin.' Emrys noticed Cowlin's sceptical look. 'You don't know everything, then, college boy? Aye, they put her in the nut house, a bloody mental institution'

'She went mad?'

'Of course not, you stupid bugger. That's what they did with them in those days, girls like Enid. The state's answer to under-age sex and unwanted kids was to lock the girl up if her family wouldn't stand by her. Get her out of sight. Out of mind. Just in case it caught on, like. It happened to more than one round here, I can tell you. Only Enid never came back out, not for twenty years she didn't.'

'That's incredible. What happened to the baby?'

'They took it from her. A little boy it was. If her people hadn't been a bit more useless than normal, they could have got her out after a few years, but they moved away and Enid got forgot. She was in that hole down the valley. It's knocked down now. That's when she was discovered again; they had nowhere to put her, see. Someone did a very late bit a hand wringing and she was released. They gave her a few quid and a bed-sit. She was *cured*. Bastards.'

'So where does Evans come in?'

'I'm getting to that. Enid got a job down Waldo's cafe. Waldo saw it as his catholic duty, which meant the girl worked all hours there for peanuts. Perfect in that place she was, didn't say nothing to the customers and done everything she was told. I tried talking to her a few times but she didn't seem to know me. Kept putting a hand over her face and looking like she wanted to bolt, like a rabbit caught in a flashlight. The looks had been washed out of her too. You could have taken her for fifty, not a woman in her thirties. All the life had been slapped out of her face.'

Emrys stopped to restock his pipe. He lit it and his face diluted into the blue haze he created.

'Enid had been with Waldo a few months when Evans come along. It was about '57, I think, 'cos there was a jukebox in there then. Evans was on the turn then, you could say. He had one of them walks, like a duck on ice, and his hair was piled up with grease. He looked like a podgy Jimmy Dean.

'Evans had a job with the council, rent collecting. He must have got going with Enid when he popped in for his frothy coffee. We were all amazed. They was together in a few months and everyone but Evans' mother knew. I'll say one thing for Evans, he brought that girl back to life. She smartened herself up, and stopped looking like a sack. She could never be pretty again, mind, but she did start to show a bit of her old figure.'

'How did he manage to get through to her?

'I asked him that myself. He didn't want to answer at first, then he mumbled something about her *being different.* Different like himself, I suppose he meant. They weren't a real couple, he said, just company for each other.'

'So what went wrong?

'What usually goes wrong for boys like Evans – his bloody mam. She had to find out sometime and when she did, Christ, what a performance. She let Evans have the full range. *He was throwing his life away. The girl was mental and a slut. What would people think?* 'Specially that one. The land of the twitching net curtains and all that. She sliced Evans up into pieces with her razor tongue, and Enid was in no state to fight her corner to hang onto Evans. She took it, like she always had.'

Emrys exhaled more clouds and reached for the last of the tea. It left a wet 'O' around his puckered mouth.

'Aye, it was another dose of shit for our Enid,' he continued. 'She left Waldo's and left the village. There was rumours that she was living rough down Cardiff, on the streets. Evans' mam, well she thought this proved her point, the old cow.'

Emrys paused and looked sharply at Cowlin.

'Look, you're not going to write all this down, are you? I still drink with Evans, after all.'

'Who would want to read it?' Cowlin answered.

'Okay then.'

'Evans spilled the real beans to me years after. It was New Year's Eve, during the miners' strike, the first one. We'd all had a good drink and I was more anxious about where he was putting his hands than listening to him; then I understood what he was saying. I should have stood up to that bitch, he kept mumbling. What you on about, I said. Stood up to who? Mam, he said, my bloody mother. It might have worked if I'd owned up, back in the thirties. He really turned on the waterworks then. I had to get him into a corner. Good job it was almost twelve, and everyone falling-down drunk. The kid was mine, Evans said, Enid's kid was mine. Ours. I looked at him daft. But I was only sixteen, he said, and scared, so I kept quiet and so did she. I didn't know they'd put her away. And then I went and destroyed her all over again when she came out. I've never bothered with women since.'

Emrys inhaled the dregs of his pipe, coughing as he wheezed out the last of the smoke, and dabbed at his rheumy eyes.

'Bloody chest,' he muttered. 'I sobered up a bit sharpish after that and got Evans home. It was never mentioned again, so you keep this to yourself an' all. It's all a long time ago now. Water under the bridge.'

Cowlin nodded as he let the old man out, then turned to his desk, like a drunk sniffing whisky, or a bear awaiting the return of the salmon. Keeping it to himself was not what he did.

BOTTWOOD M.M.

It had been some time since Pugh had told us a tale. We had heard so many over the years we thought his rich vein might be mined out, but he had one nugget left, and it turned out to be one of his best.

The village was drifting its way through a warm June day, a Sunday kind of day, a Sunday of old, that is, and the mood in the 'Spite drifted with it. A sinking down late afternoon sun added to the nicotine yellow of the pub's paintwork as Len got a round in. Pugh told him to sit down quickly.

'Len, stop swilling beer round that tray and park yourself and I'll tell you something. I'll tell you all something. I feel in the mood.'

His glare challenged us for noise but there wasn't any, just the solid tick of the wall clock, still going after so many years. Like us.

'Right then,' Pugh said, 'when I was in the army—'

There was a collective groan.

'Shut up, you haven't heard this one.'

Pugh took an envelope from his pocket, smoothed out its creases and waved it at his audience, like an exhibit in a courtroom.

'From his bloody missus, this is,' Pugh said. 'Incredible. How she even knew my address after all this time.'

Pugh waited until the table had tensed enough with anticipation. Evans winked at the others, and swept back the oiled remnants of his hair.

'Yes, this is from Bottwood's wife,' Pugh said, 'she says that crazy bastard has finally pegged it. I'm amazed he was still alive. Earnest Edward bloody Bottwood.'

Evans sniggered and muttered, 'What a name.'

'You wouldn't laugh if he was here now. Hardest bloke I ever met, Bottwood was. It was when I was doing national service, in Malaya. You know, the Virgin Soldiers. Bottwood was the only regular soldier in our platoon. The rest of us were just kids, living in fear and the hope we'd get a leg over before we copped one in the jungle. Aye, Bottwood, M.M, we called him.'

Pugh supped his beer and settled into the rhythm of his story. The group checked faces to see if this was indeed a new one. It was.

'If you lot don't know what went on in Malaya then you'll have to find out from someone else. This isn't a history lesson. Let's just say it was another bloody backwater war, when we thought we still had an empire to save. Thumping the natives in the name of freedom or some such slippery word. No one objected much in those days, except the locals. It was no place to do your national service, that's all I know.'

'Politics,' Evans snorted with disdain, but no one took any notice of him. No one ever did.

'We were stationed in Farel, in the heart of the country,' Pugh continued. 'Rotten hole it was too. They used to send us out on patrols from there, *to probe for terrorist activity*. It was a bloody fiasco. We'd go in threes. A local up front to guide us, then first scout, an experienced man, if you were lucky, then the bloke bringing up the rear with the heavy machine gun. That was me, because you had to be a bit hefty to use them buggers. Me and Bottwood were a team. You're the only bastard I can trust, he told me, on account that I was steady like.'

Pugh paused, and was obviously still proud of this ancient compliment.

'To say we were trigger-happy was putting it mildly. At the slightest sign of anything the front two would drop down and I'd spray everything in front of us with bullets. Shot a native once, that way. An accident. Christ, that jungle was a killer. Slimy, always wet, smelling like a khazi, snakes as thick as your leg, spiders big as your fist, and leeches dropping on you like greedy slugs. Everything dripped, until you felt like it was dripping inside you.

'We were fighting over a place like that, for Christsake. Some blokes went potty out there, but Bottwood was potty to start with. Everyone thought I was doing them a favour by being his oppo, but I got to like the man, even if I was scared of him. Who wasn't?'

Pugh's audience was very much a captive one now.

'Bottwood won his gong on Sword Beach,' he said, wiping the froth of his beer away from his mouth with a gnarled fist. 'It was the only medal really worth having, he told me. Any fool can get the Victoria Cross, all you have to do is die with a lot of show, but the Military Medal, that takes soldiering, and being canny enough to keep your head on your shoulders whilst you're doing it. He killed a load of Jerries single-handed, so they gave him a gong and made him a sergeant.

Made him a sergeant three bloody times and he got busted every time they done it. But he stayed in the army. Where else could he go? That's what the army is for, in peacetime anyway, to take all the crazy men from the streets. They need each other.'

'How was he such a nutter then?' Evans asked.

'I'll give you an example. To everyone's surprise, especially mine, it turned out that Bottwood was married, to a woman from Gloucester. She used to send him photos of herself – *posed* photos. She'd be wearing underwear, suspenders, cami knickers, the lot.'

The attention of the audience took on another dimension, and all drinking stopped.

'She wasn't a bad looker either, a bit beefy mind, but she'd have to be to suit Bottwood. *My little girl,* he used to call her. When he came back from the Naafi steaming, he'd get the photos and pass them round. We all knew what to say – haven't she got nice hair, Bottwood, you can tell she's a lady, that kind of nonsense. But one night a new bloke was with us, and he didn't know the score. Look at the arse on that, he said. Bottwood was on him with a bayonet. Slashed a chunk out of his arm. We all jumped on him, but he shook us off like rag dolls and chased the bloke out into the square, yelling like a banshee. He would have done for him, but the lad legged it like a whippet. Bottwood got a month inside for that, but that place was a second home for him, and even the MP's didn't mess with him. No one did.'

Pugh took a long draught of his pint, looking at the empty glass thoughtfully.

'Bottwood was a strange sod, you never knew which way

he was going to jump. He wanted us to see his wife with nothing much on, but you had to be polite about it, like it was bloody normal.'

'Perhaps it was, for him,' Evans said.

'Shut up,' Len said. 'Carry on, Pugh.'

Pugh's face creased up, furrows and dents forming a map of concentration.

'Farel was where the army used to train its guard dogs. It was the centre for that part of the world. They made vicious dogs worse, made sure there wasn't one spark of friendliness left in 'em, and the largest and nastiest brute in the compound at that time was Baskerville, a Rottweiler. Even its handler was wary of it.'

Pugh picked up his pint and the last two inches of bitter disappeared down his throat. He was satisfied he had the table hooked like a hapless trout.

'It had been a bad time for me. I still had to go out on patrol when Bottwood was in the clink, and felt naked without him. A few of the blokes had copped it in a skirmish up country. They were ambushed when they were burning villages. We did a lot of that, burn villages.'

Pugh was quiet, his mind elsewhere for a moment, and his eyes looking back into a troubled past.

'So when Bottwood got out he felt like a good piss-up,' Pugh said, taking up the story again. 'We went to the Naafi. You can pay, he said, and I did. We were the last two they chucked out, stumbling out into the night drunk as lords. It had been belting down with rain, and the heat was steaming out of the ground. Steaming out of us too. The moon was out, like a big bloody electric light. We heard shouting coming from the dog pound, then a few blokes shot past us, running like hell. "Piss off out of it," they shouted, "Baskerville's loose and he's ripped up his handler." I did try to piss off out of it but Bottwood took hold of me. "What's the matter with you," he said. "Scared?"

'You bet I was. That was the cue for the beast to appear, wasn't it? We were in an alley and it was bounding down at us from the top end. I swear I could see the moon catch in its eyes and the slaver drip off its jaw. It was almost four feet high at the shoulder but I couldn't break Bottwood's grip to scarper. It was iron. I sobered up pretty sharpish, I can tell you.'

'"Stand your ground," Bottwood said, "it's only a dog. A dumb animal. We are *men*." Bottwood had a flagon bottle of the local muck in his free hand. He let go of me just as Baskerville was about to spring, stepped to one side and smashed the brute on the side of the head as it flew past. I couldn't believe how easily he done it. The dog was half stunned but he put his foot on its neck and ground what was left of the bottle into it. Bottwood didn't believe in just wounding, man or beast. Jesus, what a sight. Bottwood standing there with his hands soaked in blood, and the dog left with a mess where its head should have been.

'Before I had time to recover I had another bloody shock. Up comes Norman, the sergeant in charge of the dogs. He pulls his service revolver, cocks it, and stands there calling Bottwood a butcher. M.M. just sneered at him, inviting him to shoot. He turned to me and said, see, see how the army values a man. Less than a bloody dog. Christ, I wish he'd left me out of it. I thought we were both going to cop it.

Norman's hand was twitching on the trigger, I could see his fingers tightening. An officer comes running up just in time. He knocked the gun out of Norman's hand with his swagger stick. All right man, he says, it's all over, and Bottwood, you're on a charge.'

Pugh held up his empty glass.

'Who's shout is it?'

No one moved, so entranced were they with the story.

'What happened to Bottwood?' Evans asked.

'I dunno. I got posted back to Blighty while he was inside. I left him the old girl's address but we lost touch, until I got this letter. Bottwood died two months ago. This came to our old address and got lost for a while. He knew he was on his way out and wanted to get in touch with his old army friends, have a bit of a reunion, like. Christ, he didn't have any friends, the poor bastard. Funny how I remember it all so clearly, but that crazy bugger taught me something in that alley. Something I've never forgot.'

Pugh paused and dabbed at his watery eyes.

'Sweat,' he muttered. 'I did write back, to his missus, that same one we used to oggle, but he was dead by then. She told me he'd tracked down all the blokes from that unit, it had become a bit of an obsession for him. I was the only one, she said, the only one who bothered to reply.'

QUIET KEITH

If any of us in the 'Spite had been asked to conjure up the most unlikely actions for Keith, no-one would have even got close to what he did. For Keith to have found a girl was miracle enough but there was no accounting for what happened afterwards. It was a sensation, that stuff in Merthyr.

Gentle dreamer, loner, and as shy as a whippet, that was Keith. He was a lanky string of a man, with a large slab of dirty blond hair that always obscured his left eye. Whatever he wore, his clothes always seemed to be trying to get away from him; he was untidy, but never scruffy. Keith was long-faced and quietly watchful, his eyes nervous and flint grey. He lived in Laura Street, with his mother, a middle terrace, the one with an aspidistra as big as a hedge in its dark passageway. Mrs Hopkins believed in tradition.

When his job in the pit went the way of all the others Keith became a regular in the 'Spite. He was the youngest retired collier in the village, but despite his youth he often seemed older than us in his ways, as if he had bypassed middle age in one fell swoop. We made him our mascot and he rounded off our table nicely. There was Evans, Pugh, Lenny and myself. Keith was our mammy's boy, if you like, harmless, but with a bit of a brain on him, and always good for a few facts.

Perhaps it was the time on his hands that procured that girl for Keith. He had taken up cycling and an interest in the old pit sites and other industrial relics scattered around the valleys. We thought him a bit cracked, bothering with the past like that, rubbing salt in old wounds. I'd see him set out early morning, if there was a bit of sun, pushing his bike up the hill, his clipped legs straining against the crumbling tarmac like two sinewy sticks. Sometimes he wore a beret and carried a notebook. By evening he was back in the 'Spite with us, supping ale and probing his paper with his fingers. He was silent and still then, for the rest of the night.

Keith met the girl on one of his cycling forays. It was at Merthyr station, where he waited for the train down, too tired to pedal home. I have often wondered how they got talking, what on earth he managed to say to her, but he must have said something, for they were inseparable in weeks. She appeared in the village one day, holding onto his arm, and Keith showing her off with hesitant pride. It caused more than a few stares, and twitching net curtains. Talk soon followed.

She was younger than him, *much* younger. A showy dresser, in short skirts, with useful hips and a tidy bosom. A tart, the village quickly judged – she had to be. A tart after his Coal Board pay out, which was not inconsiderable. Besides this female body poured into tight clothes Keith looked even more skeletal, his face winter pale next to the over-painted one of his new friend.

'She must have fancied them bike clips of his,' Pugh muttered, as the couple passed the 'Spite window.

'More like his redundancy money,' Len said. 'He must have a fair bit stashed away besides that, too. Keith was always close with the stuff, even when he was working.'

'Here,' Evans said, 'do you think they've done it, then? Is Keith up to it?'

We laughed at this, but there was also a touch of resentment in the air. Keith had disturbed the balance of the group, and jealousy stirred. How could a man like that, we asked ourselves; why couldn't men like us?

Keith brought her to the 'Spite just the once. We watched, like cats dusted with fish scales, as she flounced in, all legs and perfume, dragging a bashful Keith with her. He acknowledged us sheepishly and guided her to another table. Not too close, but close enough for us to hear snippets of the talk. It was Keith this and Keith that. She held onto his arm the whole time, like a cobra with hands.

Pugh uttered a periodic 'Duw, Duw, who'd have thought it.'

'Poor sod,' Evans said, 'she'll eat him for breakfast. Maybe she has already.'

Lucky sod, we all secretly thought.

Keith went up to Merthyr to stay with the woman. I wonder what his mother thought of that, with her chapel sniffs and I'm-better-than-you looks. She was the reason Keith was as he was. He had been brought up by a professional widow and life-hater, and had barely known his father. Mrs Hopkins was as dry as a stick and she'd kept Keith very close, like a possession. She must be aghast at developments, I thought, for there was no doubt Keith had made a dash for freedom, and his innocence had been blown away. There was jauntiness to his step now, and a new confidence in his face. It nestled there, suggesting a secret kept and shared at the same time. Yes, he had found a bit of life all right, but I'm not sure that it suited him.

Then it happened. News filtered through to the village, first in dribbles, then a quick flow.

Keith had been in a bad fight. He'd killed a man in Merthyr. Chopped his head off with a shovel.

He'd been staying with the girl on an estate there, the one with numbers for streets, the one that sprawls into concrete oblivion. Keith was coming home very early, on the first train down, running from some news he'd heard that bitter February morning.

It was news that had come as a shock, but perhaps also as a relief because it wasn't the first shock he'd had recently. Three weeks after Keith had accepted Sharlene's invitation to move in with her, she produced her two children. They'd been living with her grandmother *whilst we got to know each other,* as she put it. They were two boys, aged six and four, and each one as mad as a box of frogs. At least that was how it seemed to Keith, as he was even more innocent of the ways children than women. He had no semblance of control over them, much to the disgust of Sharlene. They terrified him, and it didn't take him long to discover he was not surrogate father material, or any type of father material.

'Where's their dad?' he asked after a while.

'Oh, that bastard fucked off years ago,' Sharlene answered. 'Don't worry, they'll think you're their dad soon.'

It all started to unravel quickly then, as fantasies usually do. And when Sharlene told him the real truth about her husband his old solitary life seemed like the Holy Grail.

The station was deserted, its lights still fighting a gloomy dawn. Deserted apart from three men. One being the husband of the girl Keith had taken up with, a man just out of prison. His existence came as a great shock to Keith.

'You bastard little worm,' the husband shouted, 'we're gonna send you down the line in a box, boy.'

Imagine the terror of Quiet Keith, nine and a half stones light, facing this gorilla intent on violence. He remembered the man's boots, Keith told me, a lot later. There was a morning gleam to them, he said, a *mourning* gleam, black, funereal, mesmeric, and they had his name on them.

Keith did the most sensible thing he could. He turned tail and ran, shrieking for help from the bare station as he did so. They chased and cornered him against a wall of an outbuilding, eagerly closing on him. Keith reached out blindly and came up with a shovel. He crashed it against the husband's head, splitting it from skull to jaw. He never forgot the surprise in the man's eyes, as he sunk down to the ground. The other two looked at their friend, then they ran too, this time away from Keith and the gory scene.

Keith leant back against the wall, semi-conscious, the shovel dripping red spots onto the hoary ground. A guard took it from him, carefully.

'I think you've killed him,' the guard said.

'I think I have,' Keith answered, the words forcing their way through his taut lips.

The guard was wrong. The husband survived. Another millimetre and Keith would have indeed killed. The court case was all the news for a time. The village doted on it, drugged by its notoriety. Everyone had a story to tell about Keith, and he would not have recognised himself in any of them. It was fortunate for him that his victim had a long and violent record and Keith's own was blemish free. He did not even go to prison. His act was deemed self-defence and he got probation and the judge's lengthy reprimand about violence.

Very Quiet Keith he became after this, as he gradually resumed his place at the 'Spite table. He never saw the girl again, or any other, but he did gain the lasting respect of the village.

'I learnt a lesson there,' was all Keith would say on the matter, after a long period of silence.

'Women,' Evans said, 'a chap like you is better off out of it.'

Keith looked at him with tired eyes, pushing back his dirty blond hair, but he would not be drawn into any more words.

THE MONEY SCOOP

'Imagine how he must have felt when he scooped that money,' Len said. 'Pound coins just minted, hordes of them piled up into a golden pyramid. Dazzled, he must have been.'

This was the start of a rare story from Len. Usually he offered the table anecdotes about his legendary prowess with women, often cut short by the derision of Pugh.

'You're a legend in your own underpants boy, and nowhere else,' Pugh liked to say, and we always laughed. You did, with Pugh.

Len's tale concerned his nephew, Leon.

'Of course you know him,' Len said, 'tall, good looking boy. Hair the colour of coal and broad shouldered too. A lot like me, in fact.'

'An odd name for someone round here,' Pugh muttered, snorting into his empty pint.

'It was the name of the Wolfman,' Len said proudly, always keen to share his very general knowledge. 'Remember, it was Oliver Reed's first snarling role. My sister fancied him, so she named the kid accordingly.'

'You sister fancied the Wolfman?'

'No, bloody Reed, mun. Anyway, exotic names are all the go now.'

Leon had won first prize in a national competition, and it

lay at the Royal Mint, ten miles down the valley. Using a large scoop he had three minutes to take his fill from a pile of pound coins. Not nearly long enough, we thought.

'You'd be surprised,' Len said. 'It was a bloody big scoop.'

'How much did he get then?' Evans asked.

'Aye, get on with it,' Pugh added. He'd returned from the bar with the beer, five pints which had shed some of their load on the journey. We all scowled at the minor lake lapping at the edges of the tray, but said nothing. Not to Pugh.

'Right,' Len said, 'Leon goes along on the day. It's all set up for him. People from the papers, officials, and that tart the dog food company got in.'

We all leant closer to the storyteller.

'That's who held the competition, see,' Len explained. 'Dog food, that advert that's always on the box. All those hounds racing around the hills.'

'I know that one,' Evans said. 'Have you noticed how they always get people who look like their dogs, or perhaps it's the dogs that look like—'

'Get on with it,' snorted Pugh.

'There was more eyes on this piece than our Leon,' Len said. 'It was Lynda Jayne, after all.'

'Who the hell's that?' Pugh demanded.

'Look, Pugh, if you keep interrupting this story will never get going,' Evans said. 'Even *I* know her, that page three girl from a few years back. Murdoch's Madonna, they used to call her, before she was struggling to stay on the right side of thirty. I saw her on a quiz show once. Stocky lass, like a triangle on heels.'

'That's sexist, that is,' Talbot muttered.

'That's the one,' Len said, 'big Lynda Jayne. She'd never been to Wales before, she told our Leon, in one of them accents that don't seem to come from anywhere.'

Len paused to down half his pint, warming to his story.

'Leon scooped away like mad, sweat dripping off him like crazy. Thirty loads he managed, and it might have been more if he hadn't kept glancing at Lynda's chest. He got eighteen thousand, four hundred and thirty two pounds with that scoop. They changed it into a cheque for him.'

'The boy came straight to our place, waving that bit of paper around like a flag. "Know what I'm gonna do, Uncle Len," he says, "go down that bloody dole office and tell them where to stick their giro." 'Course, he didn't have no choice there, not with his new found prosperity. I watched him prance his way up the street and thought he might not hold onto that money too long. My sister must have thought the same, because she got him to put it into a building society the next day.'

Len raised his voice to counter the racket from upstairs. The 'Spite now had *musical nights,* an attempt to counter hard times which only succeeded in moving thin custom around. Len was in competition with *Delilah*, sung with hopelessly misplaced enthusiasm.

'Leon had a do at his local that night, but he only bought one round of drinks. His girlfriend, Mair, saw to that. She said they had enough now to put down a deposit on a terrace, and furnish it properly, what with her job in the supermarket. This was news to our Leon.

'By ten the party was going well. Even my sister was on her way, but no one was too pissed to miss Lynda Jayne. She flounces into the pub, with two walking walls to mind her. Her agency had told her about Leon's do, and she had to stop over in Cardiff anyway, she said. Jesus, I've never seen the boys so bad. You don't expect restraint at the best of times, not when they're in drink, but when they saw Lynda it was all noses to the trough. Even Billy Hughes followed her around with his tongue dusting the floor. Like a bear sniffing out a salmon, he was. Got a bit dodgy with the minders at one point and Mair was not amused, but her complaints fell on sodden ground.

'It was strange. Lynda didn't seem to bother with Leon much, but after stop-tap, official stop-tap, that is, she was around him more, and he wasn't slow in coming forward either. Mair couldn't do anything about it because she passed out at half ten. My sister had to take her home. In fact they both threw up outside Manfredi's; caused a bit of shame in the family, that did.'

'You're not saying Leon went off with the woman, are you?' Evans asked.

'No, not then, he could hardly stand, let alone perform. No, Lynda left with the two apes. I saw them drive off in a white Mercedes and thought that would be an end to it. She'd had her night of rough.

'Leon copped it in the morning. My sister on one side, Mair on the other, a right pincer movement. But Mair came around; she had eighteen thousand reasons to. Leon escaped to our place and I poured tea into him.'

'"Thing is, Uncle Len," Leon said, "I love Mair and all that, but I dunno, it's all a bit sudden, and there's things I want to do."

'"Aye, like spend your money on yourself," I said.

'"Well okay, some of it anyway. I've never had nothing before, and I've only been seeing Mair for a twelve month anyway."

'"Six weeks was long enough for your mother," I said. But despite thinking Leon a selfish young git I did understand him. Who could blame him, wanting to break free of this place? The money had given him a whiff of freedom, but it was a whiff might lead to a greater need, and then he'd have trouble. So I didn't say anything one way or another.'

'What do you mean by *this place?*' Pugh said.

The table braced itself for an onslaught.

'Nothing, Pugh, but we're not young, are we? We've seen better times, but what's here now for boys Leon's age? Christ, they can't even get a bus down the valley after nine. Remember when we used to—'

'All right, all right. Get on with the story,' Pugh said, loud enough for the barmaid to glare at him.

'Right. Two days after the do Leon had a phone call. It was Lynda; she was still in the area. He snuck down to the motorway junction and she picked him up. She didn't have the Mercedes, or the apes. They belonged to the agency. No, she had an old Ford Escort, which should have told him something. They went down to a pub in the Vale and that's when it started. You could say Lynda cut him out from the herd, fine young bullock that he was, and a bullock with a bit of loot. Leon got his money out, and they were down Tenby that weekend.

'Mair went demented. She was round our place looking for him, crying and threatening at the same time. Blaming me, for Christ sake. Leon stayed down there 'til Monday. Know what he told me, boys, "I tasted heaven that weekend, Uncle Len." Christ, I didn't know the kid was a poet. Bet he tasted plenty of other things too. He was back, dodging Mair and getting his passport, then off again. To Bermuda with Lynda, can you believe, revving up his hire car like Fangio in a hurry.'

Len sank the last of his pint, got his second wind, and went on.

'They were out there three weeks. That's how long his dosh lasted. Lynda showed him a slice of the high life all right, and Leon paid for it. Casinos, hundred quid meals, you name it, and he bought her a necklace that cost a year's dole. I had a card from him. The sea is as blue as china, he said, every day is a daze and I don't want to ever think clear again. Poor bugger, he never have.'

'Gullible youth is at its most dodgy when it comes into money,' Evans intoned.

'Eighteen grand doesn't go far these days,' Len said.

'It would for me,' Pugh said.

'Know where Lynda Jayne really comes from?' Len continued, 'Brynamman, that's where. She's as Welsh as us lot, even speaks the lingo. She went up to London when she was seventeen, showing her big chest to the bright lights. They lit each other up for a while. That's shock number one. Second is that she didn't dump Leon when his money ran out. She wanted them to keep at it. The boy told me everything when he came home.

'"At first I was afraid to tell her the money was all gone," Leon said. "It went so fast. We blew twelve hundred in this casino she knew." All the penguins there were jabbering in French. He didn't have a clue, he told me.

"'I put the chips on where she said and it all went," the boy said. "But it wasn't just the money for her. She wanted us to stay together. You make me feel young again, she said. She went on about living in London, and getting me modelling work, stuff like that. The funny thing is, as soon as she started to talk like this, I didn't want to know. I began to see how old she was, it was a shock the first time I saw her without all her slap on. She was still well upholstered but her finish had gone. I'd blown a packet and had the time of my life and just wanted to leave it at that. I wrote to Mair and asked her to forgive me."

"'You cheeky young sod," I said, more in admiration than anger.

"'Lynda was a bit sad, when I told her," Leon said. "It was coming back on the plane. She blabbed into her pink gin, which was worse than her getting angry, and she told me her real age then. Forty bloody two. That's only a few years younger than Mam."'

'*Duw, Duw,*' Evans said. 'And that Mair took him back. Can you credit it?'

'Well, he has the looks, don't he,' Len said, 'and looks count for a lot. Mair always was a practical girl. The boy left his odd change with me before he took off, four hundred and thirty two quid, enough to buy Mair a nice engagement ring. She's got him for life now.'

'What about Lynda Jayne?' we all asked, almost in unison.
'Who knows?'

STAND BY YOUR MAN

As she sat his embalmed, partly mummified corpse upright in the armchair, it seemed to Mary that Jake was still alive. Sitting on the porch at day's end with a tumbler of bourbon on mountains of ice, his bleary, shot eyes were the red sunset, his wispy, greying hair the clouds, his bulbous, veined hands the tracks of the far horizon. She could still hear his boozy, bellowed comments too, like small claps of thunder before a storm. Her weatherman.

When Jake killed himself Mary was flying over the Mid-West, on her way to Los Angeles, for the one conference she couldn't duck. She hadn't seen it coming. There was no note, but he'd been too eager for her to go, his usual *You're leaving me again?* look absent from his creased face, as if a lifetime's self-pity had suddenly drained away from him.

She'd left him early, staring out at the warming, yellow sky, his eye glasses on his lap, like a sailor deprived of the sea, muttering about geese, herons, and sea-eagles. She'd always hated his interest in birds. Mary had never liked them much; from childhood their glassy, darting eyes had been unsettling.

That morning Mary kissed Jake on the forehead and adjusted his Yankees cap. You're still a fine looking woman, he murmured, as she was leaving. They were a couple of thirty years standing. Jake the weatherman, the once familiar T.V. face, and Mary, his doctor wife. No children.

Their Key was connected to others by a highway on stilts, a snaking curve of stone too dull to flash in the sun. Mary mused on Jake as she drove to the airport, and his last words stayed with her. There had been fire in him once; it had burned brightly in the early years, until his great interest in everything around him seemed to collapse in on itself and he became bound up by a long chain of clay-footed, unfulfilled dreams.

When she had long come to terms with her barren state, it began to bother Jake. In his forties he began to mouth about *no heir* like some fading European monarch. When they were young enough to adopt he'd said nothing; now he grew intolerable if she mentioned her sister's kids.

The station let Jake go at sixty. Their long-serving lord of weather, predictor of storms and suns and lightening, was washed up, but it was a good pay-off, and she still worked. It was necessary, for it quickly got very sticky around her man, for his attitude became as intense as the August weather, a slow burn of bitterness that seeped into his every pore. And the Florida weather was his accomplice; at this time of the year it made old chests wheeze and gasp, and every part of one drip.

Mary put in fewer hours at the hospital now. People came to the Keys to escape and to die, but they took their own sweet time doing it. Hers was not a busy practice.

Phone the hospital immediately. This was a message waiting for Mary when her plane touched down. Even then she'd not suspected, not really. When they told her, she turned round at L.A. and flew back, staring down on big country through gaps in the clouds. Endless squares of rippling greens, browns and yellows unfolding beneath her, like one of Jake's weather maps. She hummed *This Land is Your Land* to herself, bit her fingernails for the first time in forty years, and allowed her eyes to moisten.

Jake had popped two bottles of pills, and washed them down with booze, that single malt stuff he liked that cost a fortune. No room had been left for error. Mary was not the crying type, but she did cry when she saw him laid out on the slab. She hated the knowledge of her trade, knowing what they'd do to his brain, his guts, and his throat. And she also cursed him for being selfish to the end, leaving her alone on their solitary Key at the age of fifty-nine. He'd discarded a third of his life, of their lives, and left her to work out why.

Mary returned to their wood-framed house. Jake had always complained about its modest size, but now it seemed hugely empty. Sea-beaten weatherboards were arranged into a squat square; it was a period piece, looking over a flat ocean, so sluggish and unchanging at this time of year, a barely moving grey lid denying the mayhem she'd seen it churn up.

She prowled around the house, seeing him everywhere. How many times had she wished Jake gone these last ten years? Now she thought of older times, the fishing trips when he'd offered up so much of himself, when his vision was sharp, and his philosophy hopeful.

Mary made her decision when she sat in *his* chair, looking out on the sea washing up from Mexico and the boat unused for so long. Beached and up-turned like a stranded turtle. *You're not getting away that easy, Jake,* she muttered to herself.

Mary brought Jake home, patched up after his medical mauling, ready to be re-arranged once again by herself. It was difficult, but she did it, telling ridiculous lies to her colleagues about burials at sea – that Jake had become a recluse helped. What relations he had left were far away, and glad to be, and the one local undertaker melted away when she denied him the business.

So, with the right papers, and his suicide agreed, Mary got him home, using the burial at sea line on Wayne the orderly, who helped her get the body bag into the back of the station wagon. All the time telling herself that she had not cracked, that it didn't go against every scrap of sane logic she espoused, that she would not turn into one of the lost characters that stalked the Keys like loons, and that she would not be found out. Not that she was sure preserving and keeping a spouse was legal or not; there was not much precedent.

Jake would be her last practice of medicine, if embalming could be called that. She'd call it a day then, she'd have to, pulling a stunt like this. The hospital would be glad to let her go; they'd long thought her cranky, like her old man, her lateral thinking too much for the hospital's fazed clientele.

Maybe she *was* mad. Her sister Martha always said that Jake would do it to her. Leave the son of a bitch, was always her advice. But leave him for what, for whom? People on an even, well-heeled keel always played fast and loose with their advice.

The gore part was done the next day. Her stomach held.

Heart too. She'd always been interested in embalming and preserving since she was a student. On their one trip to the old world she'd dragged Jake around Egypt, waxing lyrical about hooked brains and the like, Jake protesting strongly. Now she had the very last word.

Drying was necessary. They had the perfect environment for it, and a house out of sight of the road. Not that anyone came, apart from the mailman. Jake could look out on his once loved sea, and his new eyes would not be troubled by the sun, and his Grand Canyon of a forehead crease would be smoothed out forever. Two days of messy stress and Jake was ready, somewhat desiccated and shrunken, but ready. This was Jake as she'd always wanted him to be, uncomplaining, supportive, there. His acid tongue silenced.

Mary put him in the study, which had been another place for Jake to brood in when winter came. She'd hear him chipping away at the current weathermen, deriding the daytime television he always denied he watched.

Mary finished up at the hospital as soon as she could. They held a perfunctory leaving party for her, with people who had despised Jake singing his praises the loudest. One or two asked what her future might be. Keep in touch, they said, but she doubted if *they* would.

Mary had spent thirty years with Jake. A joyful sprint to marriage, then the long unravelling of the character Jake had hidden from her. Each year had bled into the next, mocked by the slow turning of Keys life. They lived in turtle country. She'd watch them belly flop their way onto beaches, octogenarians still laying eggs. Tourists came through sometimes, their quicksilver talk cutting through the heavy air, beings from a faster world, a rushing world, Jake said. Sometimes she'd longed for rush. Mary smiled as brushed Jake's ageless hair, and re-arranged his shirt. She couldn't get that old Guthrie tune out of her head. *This man is my man.*

What's that, Jake? You'd like us to go to Europe, a long vacation. A walk through the Blue Ridge Mountains, along the spine of the east? You want a new boat? Jake, you haven't groused for a whole day, a whole week. Jake, you don't grouse any more.

Mary sat on the porch, on the new rocker she'd bought. The pelican was on its post, as it had been for twenty years, gazing endlessly out to sea. Jake had been at one with that damn bird. It was her sixtieth birthday, May Day, with the sun limbering up for another season. Mary called out to the pelican and told it so, then she poured another drink, his old drink. J.D. on an ice base. Never drink it neat, Jake used to say, for the ice draws out the sweet taste. She had never drunk it at all until recently. It was a large one, her second, and it wasn't yet midday. Mary hummed that song again, and tilted the rocker, gently mimicking the motions of waves.

Her sister, Martha, had urged her to start again, but Mary didn't want to. Sitting out on the porch was just fine. Yeah, ice cubes shivering her tongue, music in her head, Jake nearby, this was all the life she needed, all she could realistically get. Was she saying all this out loud? Maybe. So what?

Summer came on and by September Mary knew she was a lush. By October the whole Key knew she was cuckoo. It was the mailman who blew it all apart. On a whim Mary moved

Jake from the study to a position near a front window. She was drinking a lot that day and thought he'd like a better look at the sea, at the coastline he knew so well. And she'd taken to using a Walkman, which was better than having to go in to change a disc. The postman *had* knocked, he said – special delivery – but she didn't hear him. His eyes almost started out of his head and he tripped and fell down the steps as he backed away. Then he dashed for his van, craning his head for another look back.

Wassamarra, Mary said, *you know my husband.* She laughed as the van sped away. *Jake, you've made someone's day,* she shouted, *and we're on top of the world.* There was a sense of unease was at the back of her mind but she was too soused to let it step forward. By the time the cops came she could hardly stand. Or stop laughing.

OLD FRIENDS

'It's too cold for snow,' Tom said, 'far too cold. And it never snows at Christmas anyway, except on cards.'

'Nonsense. It's never too cold. Look at those clouds. They look like they've been shot through with soot. They're hanging over the quarries just waiting to unload on us.'

'Shot through with soot indeed. You should have kept up with that poetry stuff, Gwyn, then you wouldn't have to spout such nonsense at me.'

Gwyn glanced at his friend. Tom looked permanently tired these days. His hardworking life was mapped out by the lines on his face, and defined by his ruin of a nose, which was a misshapen mulberry splodge in the centre of his face. There were also a few blue scars on his forehead where he'd been caught by splinters of flint as they flew off his quarry hammer, but Gwyn could still see the boy in him, the ten-years-old Tom.

'Being eighty-five doesn't seem to agree with you,' Gwyn said.

'Is it supposed to?'

'Perhaps we've lived too long.'

'More nonsense. No one can live too long.'

'We've seen so much change, though. The quarries gone, the wives, and the children too, in a different kind of way.'

'Here we go. Good riddance to the quarries, I say. Slave labour camps they were, men hanging onto cliffs like bloody limpets in a rock pool, breathing all that dust, and the kids, well, they've moved to places with a future. Best thing they could have done.'

Gwyn knocked out his pipe into the grate. Sparks showered onto the coals in a bright constellation, and for a moment they were pins of light even more vivid than the fire, before they crashed and burned into the heart of it. He thought about a refill but put the pipe into the top pocket of his jacket, where its bulbous head joined his line of pens.

For a moment, as he stared into the fire, Gwyn saw Martha at seventeen, saw her with the keen eyes he had then, her laughing, slightly mocking face as he passed her in the street, ashamed of his shabby clothing that was covered in quarry dust. It was a ten-hour shift for him then, as apprentice to a cutter. Perched on the quarry face like a spider without a web, on one of the higher galleries that seemed to stretch up to the slate grey heavens. He lived in fear of a fall all day, and regarded the wheeling, teasing crows with envious eyes.

Tom asked him every night that summer if he was getting anywhere with Martha, and Gwyn could hardly believe it when he actually did. Tom's own courtship was more direct. He hunted Gwen down and married her before he was twenty. When Aled was born just months later Tom basked in notoriety for a while, and enjoyed a few fights.

'You're as lost in them as I am,' Tom says, 'old thoughts for old men. Come on, let's think of the future, the *immediate* future, like going down to the Red Lion. If we do get snow I can't think of a better place to be.'

'Don't you want to finish the tree?'

Gwyn nodded to the Christmas tree they had put up in the room. It was a small wooden affair, but quite stylish in an understated way. Tom had brought it back a few years ago, when he went to a German Christmas market on the annual social club outing. It was adorned with a few worn decorations, stuff that was fished out of drawers every Christmas, but this year there was a new fairy to go on the top, sent to them by Tom's granddaughter. It was bright pink and only served to highlight the plainness of the tree.

'Nah, it can wait,' Gwyn said. 'It's too small anyway. Dunno why we can't have a proper tree.'

'You say that every year. Too much mess.'

Coats, scarves and hats were put on, walking sticks procured, the widower double-take they enacted most winter nights. Tom adjusted his hat in the oval mirror in the passageway hall before he opened the front door.

'I had a letter from the lad this morning,' Tom said.

'What, your Colin? That *lad* coming up to sixty, you mean?'

'He's doing better than ever. He's got fifty people working for him out there now. Australia, ugh, I couldn't stand all that sun.'

'How would you know? You've never been further than Cardiff.'

Tom snorted his usual derision, but he secretly agreed. He'd had all the sun he wanted in Libya, Egypt and Italy. That was the type of sun that came with bullets and shells. The type of sun that beat down mercilessly as his mates burned in their tank coffins. With his bad chest Gwyn was never called up. It was the Home Guard and the quarries for him, but Tom never brought this up. It was wise not to because Gwyn had always had so much pride; it was his strength and his curse.

'Put the key safe now,' Tom says, as they step out into the street.

'Yes – *dear.*'

They made their way down to the Lion. Two bent figures moved slowly through a bleak landscape, defunct slate quarries lowering over them at impossible angles, and huddled terraces lined up in crooked array under a leaden sky. They were in a monochrome film set in which Gwyn's red anorak was an incongruous splash of colour moving slowly down the street.

Water had leaked onto the pavement outside the pub and was starting to freeze over. Tom took Gwyn's arm and guided him past it.

'Watch your step here.'

'You watch yours. You're six months older than me.'

But Gwyn was glad of the support. Tom was steadier on his pins. They slid a little on the icy road surface, then were inside the pub, into the compact snug to the left of the main bar. There was room here for three tables and a few bar stools. An open fire warmed the room, coals bright with the presence of frost on the pub roof. Here it could be another era, their era, apart from the arrival of lager, a drink that had touched their lips just once. Once was enough.

'Get them in then,' Tom said.

Other long-retired men joined them, and dominoes began. Tom smacked his pieces down on the table with a flourish, but Gwyn preferred a gentler approach, neatly linking his pieces into a chain. Chat was stilled as they warmed to their task.

The landlord put more damp coal on the fire, making the fire hiss. It competed with the clacks of the game for a while. Then the fire settled down again, and was all that could be heard was a collection of chests wheezing in unison. Four old men were hunched over the table as if they were carved in stone, looking for all the world like Blaenau's own Mount Rushmore.

'Snow's starting to come down heavy,' the landlord said, as he collected the empty glasses, of which there were more than a few.

No one took any notice of him as Gwyn won another game.

'Give the rest of us a chance,' someone muttered. Gwyn smiled as he collected his new pieces. His fingers lovingly worked against their indentations, and the once-white dots that had long since turned nicotine yellow.

The landlord was right. Outside snow was falling in a thick white wedge, and it was the right kind of snow to stick and accumulate. It soon began to drift as the wind started to re-arrange it about the town, stilling all noise. Two of the men decided to leave. They still had wives.

Gwyn accepted a large whisky from Tom, a rare drink for him, plus another pint of stout. He felt good, as his warm inner self drifted with the heat of the room. Tom suggested pontoon.

'It's a good game for two,' he said.

They had been a strange pairing in their lifelong friendship, Tom fiery, fighting his way through his youth with quick fists, but always watching out for the less hardy Gwyn. The war years were the only time they had been separated. It seemed sensible for them to share the one house when their wives died, and they were definitely the odd couple of the village now.

'Who'd have thought it, though?' Tom said.

'Thought what?'

'Women are supposed to live longer than men, aren't they?'

'Aye, so they say.'

'And us two are still here.'

There was another lapse into silence as each man sifted through his memories, arranging images into comfortable, drink-encouraged nostalgia. Tom smiled when he recalled a particular fight with Gwen, in the early days when she set about changing him. Trying to change him. His old friend was also lost in his thoughts. Perhaps we should be getting back, Tom thought. Gwyn was not too good on his feet these days but it was so comfortable in the snug, whilst their house was poorly heated, and draughts knew every trick in the book. Another half an hour wouldn't hurt.

The landlord came back in.

'Come on, boys, you're the only ones left now. Get home now before you are snowed in.'

'Stuck in a pub?' Tom said, 'doesn't sound so bad to me.'

Keri the landlord knew better than to ask them if they hadn't got homes to go to. Tom and Gwyn were fixtures in the Lion, and Keri had a perfect knowledge of their history, as all good landlords should.

'Come on,' Gwyn said, 'Keri's right.'

'Okay, okay.'

'Merry Christmas, boys,' Keri said. 'Don't go too wild.'

The landlord locked up as soon as they left, his 'Mind how you go' cut off by the closing of the pub door. Outside all was changed, and traffic noise was absent. That unique stillness a heavy fall of snow brings was all about the town, and for a moment it seemed to Gwyn that they were the only two people in the world. Their way home was now camouflaged in white.

'Christ, this is like the old days,' Gwyn said, 'remember those winters we used to have, and it's still chucking it down.'

'Better hold onto me.'

'We'll hold onto each other,' Gwyn answered, feeling safe inside his boozy cocoon. This was the best Christmas Eve he could remember since the wife had died.

They walked arm in arm, like ancient lovers, walking sticks feeling out a path like mine detectors, for there was no pavement any more, and their feet were as confused as their minds. Snow whipped into them, but the rush of the wind was cushioned now. They existed in a pocket of silence, and the town was now as quiet as a tomb. The wind hindered them, but stealthily, pushing them into furrows, against walls, sapping their energy.

'This is a bugger,' Tom said, breathing hard, 'slow going, like.'

'Takes you back, though, doesn't it? Remember how we used to love the snow?'

'All kids love the snow.'

Tom gave Gwyn a look he'd been using for seven decades, derision and affection blended into a permanent friendship. Gwyn was aware of the cold now, working on his outer fringes and wanting to get closer, into the heart of him. But there was nothing to worry about, he told himself, the house was just minutes away. Hold onto Tom and keep going was all he has to do. No problem at all, and in the morning they could celebrate Christmas, as they had done for so many years. Gwyn wondered what Tom had got him, but there was no need, for it was always the same – pipe tobacco and a book.

'We're home,' Tom said, after what seemed like a small lifetime of snail-like progress to Gwyn. 'I can feel the steps with my stick. Get the key out.'

The key. Gwyn knew he had it somewhere, deep in a pocket for safe keeping, in some cold, faraway part of him. But he had so many pockets. Which one was it? It seemed hard to think, and even harder to search his pocket.

'Gwyn, don't doze off. Gwyn, for Christ's sake. We've got to get inside.'

Gwyn felt the key now, in the right pocket of his coat, the new, small gold Yale. He pulled it out with a brief show of triumph, and lost his balance. He went over into the snow, taking Tom with him. They landed softly, just a gentle crump in the deep, white bed. Tom fell with a grunt but was otherwise silent. Gwyn reached for his friend, and managed to shake him, but Tom did not respond.

Winded, Gwyn leant back for moment. It had stopped snowing, and there must have been a break in the clouds, for he could see stars, sharp, blinking points of light. They look like white nails hammered into a black velvet background. That would make a good line for one of his old poems, he thought.

'I dragged you down, did I, Tom? Aye, must have. Sorry, Tom.'

Gwyn could still taste the whisky in his mouth, a comforting burn to keep out the cold. All these years Tom had sworn by the stuff, but he had not listened. Until now.

Gwyn waited for Tom to get him up. It was what Tom had always done. Looked after him. Not that Gwyn was worried. He was comfortable, like he was in the bed of his dreams, not like that old wrack in the house, which encouraged every niggle in his body, where turning over only lead to a cold, unused part of the double bed, making him ache with memory and loneliness. No, this was a comfort he could sink into; he had sunk into it. Gwyn tried to concentrate, and with a real effort nudged Tom again.

'Tom, are you with us? Can you get up?'

Tom stirred, and regained consciousness.

'No, I don't think I can. Have you still got the key?'

The key, Gwyn had forgotten about it. Taking it out of his pocket seemed like such a long time ago.

No,' Gwyn said, 'it must in the snow somewhere.'

'Well, bloody feel for it.'

'Feel where? It's gone.'

'Try calling for help then, I've got no breath.'

Feeling foolish, Gwyn is able to raise a few weak helps,

but the wind quickly stole them. He managed to turn towards Tom. It was seventy five years ago, on their first camping trip, when he feared snakes and just about everything else, and was glad Tom was with him. Like he was now. The stars were out, he was sure of it.

'Look at the sky, Tom. It's beautiful, like a blue-black dome pricked with sparkling pins. I wrote that when I was seventeen, do you remember?'

'Aye, and you still haven't learned to keep quiet about it.'

Gwyn regarded the immensity above him, so calm, so vast. He spread out his hands, and one closed on the key. It had been just inches away. Finding it was a triumph, and Gwyn felt as if he's bursting with it. He wanted to shout out to Tom, but he hadn't the strength. He sunk lower into the snow, into his wonderfully soft bed, and rested easy on his back as he held the key tightly in his hand. Their front door seemed like a million miles away and it might well have been. Tom was already snoring.

That blue-black dome was clear now, and sharp with frost. Gwyn knew the stars were still there, but they seemed to be going out, whole galaxies were extinguishing. He smiled, in a way he hadn't since Martha died. He wasn't sure if something was about to end or start anew, but he was ready for either.

'Aye,' Gwyn said softly, touching his old friend gently on the shoulder, 'ready. Ready for both of us.'

AT THE FOUR ACES

So Jimmy Cond takes a gun to a club to Fifty-second Street, in the hot days when the strip was jumping. That place had the usual arrangement, steps down to a low basement stuffed with sale lot furniture and a bar not big enough for a lush to lean on. Cruel lighting, shadowy corners, night people, hustlers, dealers, fixers, pimps, a lurching crowd on the make, looking for thrills, and amongst them, some even there for the music.

There's a combo up. Five pieces, fronted by a horn player who is/who's moving with the times, no, he's making the times. It's nineteen fifty-seven, be-bop has grown old, and worse, it has grown accepted. So the horn man is looking for new angles; like the crowd he seeks a new edge.

Once a burst of hard fast notes, the horn is now soft and spare; it doesn't rasp, but breathes coolly. It sounds like a man trying to get his breath, and it lives in the space between big chords. It is perfect for the night. The man is shiny sharp in his Brook Brothers suit, and cool struggle pours from his horn. He assaults his audience, seduces it, makes it think, but he doesn't care about them, and they are hooked on the brilliance of his disdain.

Jimmy Cond nods to the music. Jimmy is hip, solid, gone, a man of the street, a man of jazz. His face is a sweaty veil, his eyes hot-wired to the music. He might be a junkie, any kind of broken man, but the music holds him together. Jimmy's eyelids flicker to every nuance of the horn, he jerks as the tenor sax cuts in, his fingers tap out the bars, take in the changes. He forgets the ice of outside; for a few minutes the cold stink of his tenement room fades and he forgets the busted iron bed and leaking taps as he sucks in the music, gulps it down. Jimmy sits alone at a back table. He's twenty-seven and looks forty – on a good day.

There's a break in the set. The bass player brushes past Jimmy on his way to the slimy, malodorous washroom. Someone once pissed against the hat-check stand in protest, but nothing changed, not at The Four Aces.

Jimmy comes down off the music and remembers why he is here. He fingers the gun casually placed in his deep pocket. It is heavy and bulges against him like a steel prick, chill to his touch as he runs his fingers over it, feeling its contours like a blind man in love. It's an old snub-nosed .45, a beast he has never fired. Tear a man's head clean off, the guy at the store said. Clean off.

Jimmy Cond is at The Four Aces at ten past midnight with intent in his soul. He has been over it many times in his head, so many times. He wakes with the same hot thought each morning. It will be in the middle of the last set when he'll blow the great man away.

The combo is back, and the horn player taunts Jimmy with his fire, the depth of his heart. Jimmy has played horn for fifteen years, has slaved over it for fifteen years, but is not within dreaming distance of the Man. His own instrument is in hock, to pay for the piece and six shells.

The idea came on Jimmy without warning. It took over him, mugging him with its simplicity. The horn player had been across the road in the deli, holding court, people lapping it up, because he was the Man and they were glad to be in his shade. Why should he have it all? Jimmy thought, why the fuck should he? The thought drilled into him like a sweet, fat note.

Jimmy knew the blues; he'd suffered them much as any. A mother out on the street from his earliest recollections, bringing all the *daddies* home, white daddies, black daddies, and one time a Chinaman daddy. Some beating her to shit and back. Him too, sometimes. The Man did not know this stuff, he came from black money, a college boy, for Christsake. And he thought he owned the world. The black world. The white world. The whole world.

The combo is looser now. Tense and loose. They ride a fast tempo, short stabs of sax, spare horn. The drummer rides his skins, drives the beat through the song, cajoling, bullying, and filling space.

Jimmy edges out of his seat and threads his way through the crowd. On its fringes are the brothers, the dudes of dealing, fire-eyed in the stage lights, sharing the horn player's scorn and making it their own. At the front are college kids from uptown. Gangling rich white youth in sweaters, all going someplace. A famous actor hangs out here tonight and signs autographs for them, as he tries to steal an image for himself.

Jimmy squeezes the gun against his hip. It's ready to go, it's just begging for action. It wants him to do it. Take the Man's power, it says. Take it!

He curls his fingers around the trigger. On stage they change into a slower kick, a re-worked ballad that smokes with unfamiliar changes. Jimmy gets to the front, bumping tables, spilling drinks. He steals the attention of the horn player. His eyes scour Jimmy, take him in and spit him out. They know Jimmy, they see into his musical soul.

Jimmy is within touching distance. He feels the air move around the bass drum, hears the snap of the snare, and the reed player contest his mouthpiece. He pulls the gun, it comes up in his hand like a cannon. He soars with it, ten feet tall. The horn player watches him now. Watches *him*. And Jimmy can't do it. His sand spills out at his feet and his hands are dead. It's another wasted gig.

Someone shouts, *Look out, dude's got a gun.* Jimmy's hand is jerked up and he looses off a round. Plaster falls from the ceiling and he's going down. Bodies are crushing him. His trigger finger is snapped back. People are screaming and beating on him. The gun is slipping away and Jimmy with it. The cracks in the shot-up ceiling grow into ravines and he's dragged into their darkness.

Jimmy comes to in the dressing room backstage, blasted by a naked light bulb. As he tries to move, hands restrain him. Black hands. His vision clears and the horn player is looking down on him. For a second Jimmy thinks he's in hell.

'Let him sit up,' the man says.

Jimmy winces as he puts weight on the hand. His index finger is stiff, bent and swelling purple. It hurts. Hurts like hot hell. He looks around. The whole combo is in the room, and a few other guys.

'You're Jimmy Cond, the trumpet player,' says Al, the

Aces manager. 'I remember you at the Door a few years back. Where you been, bro?'

The horn player raises a hand and there is silence.

'Why you want to kill me, man?' he asks.

'Where's the cops?' Jimmy asks, looking around the room.

'Ain't no cops, fucker,' the drummer says. 'Man don't want no cops. We settle this ourselves.'

Jimmy sees the horn case. Green leather, the Man's name embossed in burnished gold. He tries to smooth himself out, but there is crud all over his clothes. They shrivel against the horn player's duds as the room waits for an answer.

'I wanted to kill that,' Jimmy mumbles. He shuffles his busted finger towards the horn. 'That.'

'Yeah, I know,' the Man says.

'Then why ask?'

'I wanted *you* to say it.'

Jimmy croaks three times before he manages to say, 'What you gonna do?'

'Yeah, what are we gonna do,' echoes the bass player, 'teach the ofay a lesson?'

'Nah,' the Man says, 'Jimmy is all through. He's done all he can tonight.' He motions to the others to leave. 'You know, Cond, I heard you once. Yeah, over on Fifty-third. You had something, just a tiny bit.'

Jimmy can't believe it. How was the Man there without him knowing? It doesn't seem possible.

The Man unfastens his case and takes out the horn. Fixes up the mouthpiece. Hands the horn to Jimmy.

'Play it.'

Jimmy looks at him with disbelief.

'It's not the colour of your skin, man; it's inside, mother. You've lost all your colour inside. Yours is a colourless soul. A no soul. Play it now or you're fucked for all time. You don't need that finger. Use the pain, mother. Feel like you did when you pulled that piece out there.'

Jimmy is too tired to think any more. It seems like forever he's been sliding into an abyss; self-pity has polished its sides on the way down, and the monkey on his back never stops jabbering at him. Now he's touched rock bottom. He takes the horn, traces its name with his fingers and takes his stance, standing up like a shaken reed. The Man stands back, panther-lithe. Jimmy loves him. He knows it now.

Jimmy gathers himself up, pushes some air through the horn. At first it's thin and weak-toned, the Jimmy he knows and loathes. Then he hits it. Big, fat and sweet. The room fills with the rich emptiness of him. The Man stops him.

'Enough. Like I said, just a little bit. Gimme back my horn.' As Jimmy hands over the horn the Man gives him back the coat that was ripped from his back. 'Get your piece out of hock and go out the back way, Jimmy Cond. Not all the brothers have my philosophy, dig? Disappear for a while, and play again. You ain't got nothin' else, man, none of us have.'

Jimmy goes out through the service entrance, scattering trashcans and skinny cats. They wail at him but he doesn't hear them. There is ice in the air, drifting up off the Hudson to get into your bones, but he doesn't feel it. He feels the pain from his finger though. It puts a charge through him, a magnificent, exhilarating charge. Jimmy lights up a cigarette at the third attempt, sucks it into his wasted cheeks and puts a hand in the pocket where the gun was. It's changed into a wad of dollar bills.

Cockatrice Books
Y diawl a'm llaw chwith

The cockatrice is hatched from a cockerel's egg, and
resembles a dragon the size and shape of a cockerel. The
English word is derived from the Latin *calcatrix*, but in
Welsh it is called *ceiliog neidr*: 'adder-cock.' Its touch, breath
and glance are lethal.

There is a saying in Welsh, *Y ddraig goch ddyry cychwyn,*
which means, 'The red dragon leads the way.' The
cockatrice spits at your beery patriotism.

www.cockatrice-books.com

FIVE GO TO SWITZERLAND AND OTHER STORIES
NIGEL JARRETT

A daughter curious about her widowed father's love life; a woman survivor of domestic abuse; a wife who learns something startling about her jazz-loving husband at his funeral; an old actor facing memory loss; a couple whose son was executed by militants; a black American academic on a stressful stay in Wordsworth country; an early 20th-century scullery maid being taught to read by a sinister manservant... and more.

In his fourth short-story collection, award-winning writer Nigel Jarrett disturbs the clear, slow-flowing waters of ordinary lives to reveal their complications and unresolved tensions.

'Here are vivid and vital stories that crackle like bushfire and ignite delight... I read them with unbridled pleasure and holy envy.'

Jon Gower

'Jarrett's stories take seemingly ordinary or innocent situations and gently tease out their emotional complexity.'

Lesley McDowell, *Independent on Sunday*

OF THE NINTH VERSE

A. L. REYNOLDS

Anwen and her younger brother, Idwal, are inseparable almost from birth. The childhood they share involves harvesting the hay and looking after the newborn lambs in the Conwy valley, though Anwen sees before her the promise of a degree in Edinburgh or Durham and a career as a mathematician, while Idwal seems destined by his strength and skill to take over the running of the family farm. Then, as Idwal's and Anwen's feelings for each other grow darker and more complex, she finds herself put to a terrifying choice.

With a luminous prose that reflects the richness of the Conwy Valley, A. L. Reynold's novel explores both the violent, destructive force of passion and the fragility of the human heart.

Of the Ninth Verse has a profound and rooted authenticity that convinces and enchants – an enthralling novel by a writer at the peak of her powers.'

Jim Perrin

a subtly-written, compelling narrative of forbidden yet irresistible love.

Angela Topping

SEASIDE TOWNS

A. L. REYNOLDS

For Anatoliy Yetvushenko, émigré and physicist, it should be the perfect holiday. Llandudno calls to his mind the Black Sea holidays of his childhood in Ukraine, while his companion, Francis, is just beginning to awaken to the possibilities of male sexual love in the first years following its legalisation. But Anatoliy has memories of an earlier holiday in Lyme Regis in the 1950s, where his previous lover, who now lives near Llandudno, left him to make a loveless marriage. With its awareness of the landscape of the north coast of Wales, of quantum physics and of deep time, this novel reflects the search for intimacy and fulfilment in the shadow of political tyranny and sexual persecution.

A chronicler of the region's disappearing heritage

North Wales Chronicle

PUGNACIOUS LITTLE TROLLS
ROB MIMPRISS

In his first three short-story collections, Rob Mimpriss painstakingly mapped the unregarded lives of Welsh small-town and country-dwellers. In Pugnacious Little Trolls, he combines the skill and quiet eloquence of his earlier work with confident experimentation, with stories set among the bird-bodied harpies of Central America, among the dog-headed Cynocephali of Central Asia, among humanity's remote descendants at the very end of the universe, and in the muddle of slag-heaps and job centres that H. G. Wells's Country of the Blind has become. In the three stories at the heart of the collection is Tanwen, idealistic and timid, embarking on her adult life in the shadow of global warming and English nationalism.

Where is the Welsh short story going? Wherever Rob Mimpriss takes it.

John O'Donoghue

bathed in white fire in every sense... Borges would happily own them.

Gee Williams

freely and fiercely inventive short stories... supercharged with ideas

Jon Gower, *Nation Cymru*

THE SLEEPING BARD
ELLIS WYNNE
with an introduction by Rob Mimpriss

Three nightmare visions of the world, of death and of hell.

The anonymous poet is dragged from sleep by the fairies of
Welsh myth, and rescued by an angel is taken to see the
City of Doom, whose citizens vie for the favour of Belial's
three beautiful daughters; to the realm of King Death, the
rebellious vassal of Lucifer; and finally to Hell itself, where
Lucifer debates with his demons which sin shall rule Great
Britain.

   First published in 1703, this classic of religious allegory
and Welsh prose combines all the blunt urgency of John
Bunyan with the vivid social satire of Dryden and Pope, and
is published in the T. Gwynn Jones translation of 1940, with
an introduction by Rob Mimpriss reflecting on its political
significance as the union of England and Scotland comes to
an end.

Printed in Great Britain
by Amazon

86593048R00140